DIVISION MANEUVER
—THE HERO REINCARNATED—

It was like they were dancing,
spinning round and round, their swordplay
alternately furious and elegant.

It was Okegawa Kuon.

He'd come.

She had no words.

MOTEGI RIN

Childhood friend of Hanabi's, currently her teammate. Loves to tease Hanabi.

"No, you're not to blame. That was my oversight."

"Hanabi's a big fan of the Hero. She really looks up to him."

"I'll do whatever it takes to make Kuon-sama into a great Maneuver Cavalleria!"

FUJI JINDO

Squad leader to Hanabi and Rin. Earnest and good at his job.

NSR250R-SE92

a.k.a. "En". A specialized AI provided by Kaede. Supports Kuon.

SUZUKA HANABI

The girl said to be the strongest at Jogen Maneuver Academy. Called the Warrior Princess behind her back.

OKEGAWA KUON

Reincarnation of Suzuka Hachishiki, the Hero. Once Division 5, he's now Division 1—lower-ranked than the average citizen.

"Those eyes, that dumb face, that magic... You're exactly like that idiot student."

"My heart is dancing, Okegawa Kuon-kun."

"Nice to meet you. I'm Okegawa Kuon. Division 1."

NANAHOSHI KAEDE

Master to Kuon (and Hachishiki), said to be humanity's strongest woman. Also the headmaster of Jogen Maneuver Academy.

CONTENTS

SHIPPO SENOO PRESENTS
DIVISION MANEUVER

DIVISION MANEUVER

VOLUME 1

STORY BY

Shippo Senoo

ILLUSTRATED BY

Nidy-2D-

Seven Seas Entertainment

DIVISION MANEUVER VOL. 1 - THE HERO REINCARNATED

First published in Japan in 2017 by Kodansha Ltd., Tokyo.
Publication rights for this English edition arranged through
Kodansha Ltd., Tokyo.

Seven Seas books may be purchased in bulk for promotional,
educational, or business use. Please contact your local
bookseller or the Macmillan Corporate and Premium Sales
Department at 1-800-221-7945, extension 5442, or by
e-mail at MacmillanSpecialMarkets@macmillan.com.

Follow Seven Seas Entertainment online at
sevenseasentertainment.com.

TRANSLATION: Andrew Cunningham
ADAPTATION: Dayna Abel
COVER DESIGN: KC Fabellon
INTERIOR LAYOUT & DESIGN: Clay Gardner
PROOFREADER: Stephanie Cohen, Kris Swanson
LIGHT NOVEL EDITOR: Nibedita Sen
MANAGING EDITOR: Julie Davis
PRODUCTION ASSISTANT: CK Russell
PRODUCTION MANAGER: Lissa Pattillo
EDITOR-IN-CHIEF: Adam Arnold
PUBLISHER: Jason DeAngelis

ISBN: 978-1-64275-058-4
Printed in Canada
First Printing: June 2019
10 9 8 7 6 5 4 3 2 1

Prologue

TEN YEARS HAD PASSED since the Jave, humanity's natural predators, had first appeared.

_/////////

"Hero, are you gonna die?" I asked.

An oversized moon shone down upon us. We were surrounded by fires and rubble and so many bodies.

The Hero put his hand on my head, smiling awkwardly. "You're going to live," he said.

"Just me...?"

"Yes. We, at least, have to..."

"But... But everyone else is dead..."

Blood and guts were littered all around us. Some were the remains of people gobbled up by the tentacle monsters, and some were bits of the tentacle monsters left after the Hero had arrived and torn them apart.

"That's why you need to live," the Hero said. "For all those who didn't."

"You're not coming with me?"

"Sorry. I can't."

"Why not?"

The Hero looked up at the giant moon hanging overhead in broad daylight. It was pitch black, glowing around the edges. It was also a door leading to the world on the other side, a demonic moon which spit out an endless stream of the tentacle monsters that came to eat us.

A Gate...

To their nest.

"I've got to go avenge everyone."

"Take me with you!" I cried.

"I can't do that."

"They... They're all dead! Please! I want to die with them! I want to go where they are!"

"I'm sorry..." he apologized, like it hurt to say. The Hero put something in my hands and said, "Division Maneuver, activate."

Instantly, I was surrounded by a cocoon of pale light. I began floating. He was going to send me away, all alone.

"Hero!"

"This is my gift to you. Get out of this place."

"Wait, please! Don't leave me alone!"

"Goodbye. Be well."

The cocoon of light around me rose toward the sky, floating away from the imperial capital.

"Hero! Hero! Herooo!"

I yelled until my voice grew hoarse, but my cries didn't reach him. The massive black moon grew further and further away.

The Hero never looked my way.

_//////////⌐

There once was a man named Suzuka Hachishiki. He was a Maneuver Cavalleria, Squad Leader of the Suzuka Squad, First Mobile Unit of the Imperial Air Force/City Defense Corps.

Colloquially, he was known as "the Hero"—the man who had killed, slaughtered, and massacred his way through the monsters from another world.

His parents had been killed by the Jave. An orphanage took him in, but the Jave killed the nuns and all his friends there as well. Those monsters had even slaughtered his comrades in the army. In retaliation, he led missions that were tantamount to vengeance-fueled suicide, but he survived, saving the lives of many in the process and earning himself the name of "Hero".

His life was war. He was a demon who existed only to slaughter the Jave.

Now, Hachishiki was adrift in darkness. He was bleeding everywhere, on the verge of blacking out, moments from death.

After saving the girl, he'd plunged into the Gate over the capital, fought his way through mankind's mortal enemies to the Jave Queen, and...

...they'd destroyed each other.

Worth it, he thought.

He'd thrown everything he had at her. Even then, he'd been unable to win. The only option remaining to him was to use a skill that sent his magic into overdrive, turning him into a lethal storm. This skill was part of the Shichisei Kenbu, which Hachishiki practiced.

Certain of victory, the enemy queen had been just about to swallow Hachishiki whole...and took the full brunt of his attack. When he saw the Queen's flesh dissolving, he knew her body had only been held together with magic.

Yet, at the same time...

What...?

Fear sent a chill down his spine. He wasn't afraid of his approaching death. No, he'd made contact with the Queen's magic. As the Queen's body dissolved, her soul melting away, it had briefly mingled with Hachishiki's own magic.

What...is this...?!

In that magic, he sensed a terrifying degree of hatred for humanity. They'd devoured all the humans on their own world, but that hadn't satisfied them. Driven by a dark, murky, bottomless well of rage, the Jave had blown a huge amount of magic opening a Gate so they could come to this world and exterminate mankind here.

And that wasn't all...

They're... They're coming back...?!

The Queen had fled.

Hachishiki knew she had opened a Gate back to the Jave home world and flung the Core, her heart, back through it. The time would come—in less than twenty years, perhaps—when the Queen's wounds would heal, and she would return to our world.

This was bad.

He was going to die here. That was inescapable. His sight had gone, and his consciousness was fading. He had no way of warning anyone.

Please, Master! he prayed to his former mentor. *Raise strong Cavalleria, warriors every bit as strong as I was, so that, one day, when the Queen returns, they can...they can...*

Oh...

Hachishiki's thoughts grew scattered, his very being fading into the dark.

"Hero, are you gonna die?"

Where had he heard that?

Right. That girl he'd saved. It seemed like such a long time ago... Did she get away safely? He hoped she would grow up to be strong.

Hachishiki lost consciousness. It felt the same as his eyelids closing just before falling asleep in a darkened room.

Thus, the Hero perished...

DIVISION MANEUVER

CHAPTER 1

The Hero Reincarnated

ND THEN he woke up.

...Flesh tones swam before his eyes, the body of a woman he'd never seen before. The front of her shirt was undone, and she cradled him in her arms, smiling down at him. He felt so warm.

For some reason, he was certain she was his mother.

Was his life flashing before his eyes? Was he dredging up memories from when he'd been a baby? Maybe the Gate had sent his mind alone back into the past and he was hungry hungry hungry.

Hmm.

It was hard to think straight.

"Oh!" the woman said, overjoyed. She glanced at the man next to her. "Takkun, Kuon just looked at me! Heheheh."

"No way, Yuki-chan. Oh, he did! Never seen a baby focus like this. He must be a genius."

A placid wife and a childish husband; they seemed like a nice young couple. Wait, who was Kuon? Also, he was hungry. So hungry.

"Okay, Kuon. Time to eat!"

Yay!

The wife, Yuki-chan, pulled him to her breast. Food! Food!

"Drink up, Kuon! It's all for you!" the husband said.

"You're not the one making it."

"Good point! Ahaha!"

They both laughed. How sweet.

Who was Kuon?

...

No, he got it. He'd figured it out by now. He just...didn't want to jump to any conclusions. It was awfully hard to believe. Had he... Had he really been reborn as a baby?

Why? How? What for?

He didn't know. He didn't know. He didn't know.

And not knowing was uncomfortable and frustrating.

Before he knew it, he had begun crying, the ultimate battle technique only babies could use.

Surprised by the sudden change in their son (probably a son), his mother and father set to work trying to soothe him.

He couldn't control his body or his thoughts.

No good. This was too hard to think about. His brain was too new for it. He had to focus on what he could do right now.

And that...

Was drinking a lot of milk until his tummy was full, then he fell asleep.

He felt more peaceful now than he'd ever felt in his entire life.

Then again, his life had only just begun.

One day, massive holes in space opened around the world. Later known as "Gates," these are portals linking our world with the one the Jave come from. In the decades since these Gates opened, the Jave have continuously poured through them.

Possessing conical bodies primarily colored a dark purple, these hideous creatures have countless mouths and tentacles. Each Jave boasts a total length of several meters, and their tentacles grab humans, whom they then consume whole. They make nests near the Gates and lay eggs, increasing their numbers on our side.

One day, a Gate appeared above Tokyo, the imperial capital.

There were no warnings, no time to prepare.

Before the imperial government and armies could do anything, the heart of the Japanese Empire had been conquered. Aircraft were quickly reserviced to evacuate key government personnel and military leaders, taking off as soon as they were loaded.

The majority were shot down by the Jave.

The Imperial Air Force sent its Maneuver Cavalleria to the scene, Suzuka Hachishiki among them. Even when all his companions had fallen to the invaders, he fought on alone, until...

—Excerpt from *Portrait of the Hero*.

_//////////⌐

If you looked at a map, you'd see a semicircle of islands stretching across the Pacific from the Empire's mainland to the Southeast.

Those were the Jogen Islands.

Survivors of the Jave attack on the capital evacuated and settled on those southern islands, and that was where Okegawa Kuon was born, inheriting the soul of the former Hero.

By the time he was two, he was gradually learning to speak. His first word was "choco," for "chocolate." He'd loved it in his previous life, but rarely managed to get any during the war.

His next word was "Gate."

There was a saying that words hold power. Even if that wasn't true, saying things aloud could remind you of your purpose.

At two years and four months old, Kuon had realized the meaning of his rebirth.

He, Okegawa Kuon, had been reborn to kill the Queen when she returned. To drive the Jave out of our world for good.

Maybe because he'd come in contact with the Queen's soul back in that Gate, he had a sense of how much time he had until then.

Twenty years. That was roughly how long it would take the Queen's wounds to heal.

Two years and four months had already passed, so he only had seventeen years left. He had to make himself strong by then.

In his past life, Hachishiki had lost. Even with the Hero's magic level, he'd been unable to win. He'd failed to take out the Queen for good, allowing her to escape.

This was now the life where he had to finish the job.

Okegawa Kuon swore an oath, staring at his chubby little two-year-old palm. His parents squealed about how noble he looked, snapping a ton of pictures, and he struck the coolest pose he could manage, the attention not entirely unwelcome.

To kill the Queen, he needed strength.

He needed a Division Maneuver.

The world's primary combat weapon, its effectiveness against the Jave had proven to be the salvation of mankind. In his previous life, he'd enrolled in his homeland's air force and became a Division Maneuver pilot (a Maneuver Cavalleria). His unparalleled talent had made him their ace.

He had to pilot one again. There was no other way for him to kill the Jave Queen.

Right, Kuon thought. *First off, I need to tell them I'm the Hero.*

But that was the hard part. Nobody believed he was Suzuka Hachishiki's reincarnation. "I'm the Hero born again!" he told his mother, and she just laughed. "Kuon wants to be a hero!" She didn't take him seriously. He got angry and tried explaining it logically, but he couldn't put it into words, so all he could manage was, "It's true! I'm the Hero!"

He could think it, but he couldn't communicate it. It was frustrating. Was it always this hard being a child? That was a depressing thought. He ate dinner and forgot about it.

Meanwhile, he learned something from watching Jogen TV.

Thanks to the Hero, no Gates had opened in the last few years. The Gate above the capital was one of several Gates in the Empire, but all were covered in a dark mist which prevented anyone from seeing inside. Occasionally, stray Jave would appear nearby, but these were quickly exterminated by the Maneuver Cavalleria. Mankind was currently living in relative peace.

The million or so residents displaced from the capital to the Jogen Islands were growing accustomed to life there.

On these islands, they no longer gathered orphaned children and trained them to be Maneuver Cavalleria the way they had with Hachishiki. It seemed they were training Cavalleria on a volunteer basis, preparing for emergencies.

They were now the military elite, as becoming a Cavalleria afforded you any number of privileges within the Empire. In emergencies, you'd be sent into battle, but experts said it would be a while before the capital's Gate reopened. Even children thought the Division Maneuver looked cool.

For that reason, several children began receiving training to be Maneuver Cavalleria from a very young age. Kuon was part of that first generation.

When the Queen returns, I'll kill her, destroy the Gate, and banish the Jave from our world, he thought.

To do that, he had to get his new body accustomed to the Division Maneuver. His arms and legs were still short, and he had little to no muscle, but childhood had given him one advantage: He was quick to learn. If he trained hard now, he could be even stronger than he'd been in his previous life.

It was no dream; it was a firm belief with a clear purpose.

On his fifth birthday, Kuon begged his parents (on his hands and knees, which they mistook for a hilarious new game) to take him to the Division Maneuver training grounds so they could buy him a junior frame.

However, when Kuon pointed to the frame he wanted, a man in a white lab coat shook his head. "Okegawa Kuon-kun, I'm afraid you're unable to operate this."

The frame hanging in the functionally-designed hanger was a special one that stood out from the other junior frames. It was a Division 5 frame.

Kuon didn't get it. He felt like he was being told to stop at a green light.

"This happens a lot," the scientist said, scratching his head. Perhaps he just assumed all children went for the strongest-looking frame.

But he was the Hero, Suzuka Hachishiki, born again!

Oblivious to Kuon's confusion, the scientist pointed to the mountain of mass-produced frames to the left, then past those to the beat-up old frames lying in a corner out of the way. "Your magic level is 1. That's only good enough for those old ones. As long as you're just walking around."

It took Kuon quite a long time to understand these words, process them, and understand the predicament he was in.

Wait, he thought to himself. *Calm down. Take it one step at a time.*

Humans had life energy—magical energy—and they used that to operate Division Maneuver. One's magic capacity was set at birth and was impossible to increase later in life. This value was called the Potential Magic Value.

Suzuka Hachishiki's value had been abnormally high. Most humans in the world were Division 2 (Magic Value 10-99). If you were Division 3 (Magic Value 100-999), you could brag about it at school. Division 4 (1000-9999) was so rare there were probably fewer than a hundred in the entire Empire. Hachishiki's Magic Value had been 88,888, which made him the highest possible Division: 5. At the time, he was said to be the only one.

Your Division determined the functionality of the Division Maneuver—your raw strength. The stronger your magic value, the more magic you could produce, and you could operate stronger, more advanced frames. Those with very little magic had a low power output and could only operate low spec frames. To be a Cavalleria, you had to be Division 2 or above. They didn't even *make* frames a Division 1 could operate.

Then... Then I can't be a Cavalleria, Kuon realized. *So why was I reborn?!*

If he wasn't a Cavalleria, he couldn't defeat a single Jave, let alone close the Gate. He'd suffered through early childhood for five long years and had thought he could finally, *finally...*

He felt a burning behind his nose. Five-year-old Kuon tried standing up to the wave of emotion, but there was no holding it back. He was a man, a Hero reborn; he'd been alive longer than either of his parents; but those words crashed against the levee with such force they soon broke through.

Kuon cried, howling like a little baby again.

No other children were this upset by it. The scientist freaked out a bit. He could handle sulking, but full-on crying clearly made him panic.

Then, a very small woman came walking by, her words like a whip. "Don't cry, you fool."

No words wasted, no mercy shown. A phrase polished like she'd said it hundreds, even thousands of times. But that was all it took to stop Kuon's tears in their tracks, even though he'd been too young to control them himself. This verbal attack carved its way into his very soul.

Kuon spun around to see...

... a pair of boobs, attached to a woman who definitely looked like she belonged in junior high. She had a baby face, petite frame, short black hair, and was rocking a tiny suit that must have been custom tailored. When she put a hand on her hip and puffed out her chest, her nonsensically-huge breasts jiggled.

Were... Were these loli big boobs? Kuon thought. *No, wait...she looks like a little girl, but she's definitely already gone through pu—*

"Yo, little brat. You aren't thinking any dumb crap about my life experiences, are you?"

How did she know?!

Kuon realized suddenly that he knew this girl—or rather, Suzuka Hachishiki had. He knew exactly who this murderously scowling dynamo was.

"Master?"

She was Hachishiki's former master, Nanahoshi Kaede.

Hachishiki had found Kaede intolerable, worse than any demon or devil or Jave. She was the most powerful Cavalleria mankind had, the master of Shichisei Kenbu.

Kuon stared up at her, mouth open. Kaede looked him over.

"Those eyes, that dumb face, that magic... You're exactly like that idiot student."

He thought his heart would stop. "Master! It's me! I'm Hachishiki!"

At last he'd found someone who would understand he was the Hero reborn, and it was his former master. If he explained what was going on and got her on board, she could solve everything.

But Kaede put her hand on her chin, fixing him with a look of deep suspicion. "You don't say?" She snarled like a loan shark in an old movie. "Hachishikiii? Dunno any Hachishiki. Who's that again?"

"Suzuka Hachishiki! Your best student!"

"Suzuka Hachishikiii? You can't mean *him*. That idiot ignored what I said, and I had to kick his ass out."

"Yes! That same idiot!"

"...Is you?"

"Yes!"

Kaede's eyes turned to ice. Her tone was every bit as frosty. "Right..."

Kuon shivered, every inch of him trembling. He didn't know why, but he was convinced he was moments from death.

"Right, Hachishiki. There is one thing I never tried with him."

He didn't dare ask what.

"Kuon!"

As Kuon stood paralyzed with fear, his mother came running. *Saved in the nick of time*, Kuon thought. But when she realized he was talking to humanity's strongest Cavalleria, she started talking for him. He stood frozen stiff, listening to their conversation like it was happening very far away, too scared to speak himself.

"Nanahoshi-san, my boy wants to be a Cavalleria. He's Division 1, but he insists he's going to be a hero."

At this, Nanahoshi Kaede looked down at Kuon and smiled. "Fascinating."

Her smile was terrifying.

He didn't know why, but once again, he was certain he was about to die.

_//////////

...*his innate magic value meant that Hachishiki was given the strongest frame the Empire had. He was also given the best master around and was the only student Nanahoshi Kaede ever took. Although she was Division 4, she was known as the Demon God, the strongest Cavalleria the Imperial Air Force had.*

Shichisei Kenbu:

Martial arts designed to make use of magic while piloting a Division Maneuver were collectively known as "Machine Fencing." Shichisei Kenbu was one school of Machine Fencing. Widely considered the strongest of them, the arts it taught were like magic spells.

Tensetsu used the Division Maneuver to amplify your magic, using it to alter one's perception of time so everything appeared frozen. Chijin created a force field at one's feet, using it to move the user and field so quickly it was almost like teleporting. Ryusui combined the two with a sword draw.

Personality conflicts caused Hachishiki to leave his master, but, armed with mankind's greatest magic value and strongest sword arts,

Suzuka Hachishiki became a demon who existed only to hunt the Jave.

His final destination: the Gate which had appeared over Tokyo.

His final goal: to destroy that Gate, dying in the process.

Suzuka Hachishiki longed for death, to go out in a blaze of glory like the twelve companions who'd flown out with him that day and were shot down by Jave. They were killed just like all the Cavalleria who'd enlisted in the air force when he had; like the kind nuns at the orphanage; like the other orphans he'd fought with, made up with, laughed with, vowed to grow up with, and called family; like the mother and father he couldn't even remember. Suzuka Hachishiki was ready to join them.

The Hero was looking for a place to die.

Relying on his natural-born talent, he'd thought nothing of plunging headlong into the thick of enemy forces. For anyone else, this would be suicide, but, fortunately (or unfortunately), Suzuka Hachishiki was a genius. He always survived, setting new records for monsters slain, and the lives of allies were saved as a result.

Thus, he became the Hero.

This never made him arrogant, but neither did it afford him the opportunity to change his approach.

That was why his master had kicked him out before he learned the school's ultimate art. Nanahoshi Kaede was notoriously opposed to the very concept of self-sacrifice. Machine Fencing was designed to keep you from dying, so using it in pursuit of death could only lead to expulsion...

—Excerpt from *Portrait of the Hero*.

_/////////⌐

A week later, Kuon learned that what Nanahoshi Kaede had never tried giving Hachishiki was a proper scolding.

This was his first practice session. After discussing things with his mother, Kuon had become Nanahoshi Kaede's student, just as he had in his previous life. More accurately, he'd been enrolled in the private school she'd opened, and was currently the only student.

Right now, they were in an outdoor training area Kaede had set up. Like a proper class, it began with instructions from the teacher.

"I hate the Hero," Kaede stated. "I also hate the army for forcing everything on him alone. I loathe the world itself for idolizing a single man and making him fight for them. More than anything else, though, I despise that misguided fool for not valuing his own life and running off to die. We don't need a Hero like that. Don't you agree, Suzuka Hachishiki?"

"You're right."

"So, you're Suzuka Hachishiki reborn or something?"

"I am," Kuon said.

He never considered anything but an honest answer. The fear of Kaede he'd inherited from his previous life—the result of her instruction—had left him incapable of lying to her.

Kaede shot him an ear-splitting grin and made him kneel before her. She then gave him a five-hour lecture. This was clearly the karma he'd earned in his past life. His failure to live a virtuous life had come back to haunt him. He had to endure it.

The gist of Kaede's lecture went like this:

Five years had passed since Hachishiki's death. Kuon had been born at approximately the same time Hachishiki died. Although Kaede never allowed a student to return after she expelled them, she figured that, since Hachishiki had died, she wouldn't count that against Kuon.

Hachishiki was an idiot for flying into a zone after the order to retreat, a big idiot for plunging into the Gate, and a total idiot for using a self-destruct art and dying. If he ever tried that again, Kaede would turn his ass to ash, put it in an urn, and strap it to a rocket before shooting it into the sun so he'd never come back to life again.

Then, she gave him a big hug. Kuon found his little five-year-old head trapped between breasts both noticeably larger than it.

"Good job coming back, you nitwit," Kaede said, tears leaking from her eyes.

He'd never heard her cry before. Kuon once again realized just what an idiot Suzuka Hachishiki had been. He would have to spend a while relearning what really mattered. He still had plenty of time.

That was the first and last time Nanahoshi Kaede was ever soft on her student.

Machine Fencing was all about donning Division Maneuver and using your magic. Shichisei Kenbu was a school of Machine

Fencing. It was fundamentally designed for those not magically gifted. Understanding this was how Kaede had become mankind's strongest Cavalleria despite being a Division 4.

"You fool."

During his fourth training session, Kuon had engaged in a mock battle with Kaede. He was wearing a practice Division Maneuver; she wasn't. She'd utterly defeated him. He was lying in a heap on the floor, receiving the gift of her lecture.

"God. You always did just try and force your way through everything, drowning in your own natural magic ability. I'm so, *so* glad to see death didn't make you less stupid. Listen, I'm here to drill how the not-so-gifted fight into you once more. Weep or rejoice, because, from today forward, you're going to be living in Hell. Feel free to be afraid—it'll make you stronger. Faaar stronger than when they called you the Hero."

There's no way I could be stronger than a Division 5, he thought. Kuon was lying face-down on the ground, exhausted from his first DM fight in five years. He summoned the last ounce of strength he had and rolled over. The unit was already disengaged, and the plugsuit he wore was soaked with sweat.

The sky was blue, with no black Gates obscuring its endless expanse. As he lay there, belly exposed, something landed on his nose.

It was a little fairy. There was no other word that described it.

"It's an honor to meet you, Kuon-sama," the fairy said. She bowed her head.

"Master... I'm seeing things."

"You aren't! I'm your Guide, an AI Device!"

"Seriously...?"

"Seriously, Kuon-sama." The fairy Guide smiled. It was a female model, wearing a uniform that looked like a modified silk kimono. It somewhat reminded him of the conductors on local train lines.

AI Devices were magically linked to their owners. They were certainly useful, but they also burned through magic quickly and weren't in widespread use. Even Division 4s were reluctant to use them.

"Aren't they hard to use...?" he asked Kaede.

"One of the Shichisei Kenbu ultimate arts is a breathing technique that reduces magic expenditure by 1 *kei*," she replied. "I know a certain idiot who got himself kicked out before he learned it."

"What's a *kei*?"

"Ten quadrillion."

Good lord. He really *had* been an idiot.

"That Guide's yours. Don't worry, the magic is still linked to mine."

That meant it would be running on his master's magic, and all the info the Guide obtained would be sent back to her as well.

"So...it's monitoring me?"

"Remote teaching," Kaede corrected.

Well, that's one way to look at it.

"I might run a school, but it ain't open every day. I'm a busy woman, and it's all your fault."

"My fault?"

"The Queen's coming back in fifteen years. Now that I know that, I can't exactly enjoy my retirement."

Kuon didn't dare point out that that was hardly his fault. He'd already told Kaede all about the end of his previous life. She was putting many things into motion to prepare for what was to come, but...

He scrambled back up. "Master, is there anything I can do? We've only got fifteen years till they come back! So little time!"

"Don't rush it, idiot. It's the other way around. We've got fifteen whole years. We're gonna plan this thing out and be waiting for 'em."

"What kind of plan? Can I help—"

"You focus on training. You're so damn weak...*snerk*."

"Ngggh..." Kuon knew his own weakness better than anyone. He didn't need her snorting at him about it.

"When you can't come here, do what that Guide says to train yourself. Don't forget to rest. I'll know if you rush it and overwork yourself."

"Right..." He nodded, and the Guide smiled at him.

"I'll do what I can, Kuon-sama!"

"Mm. Thanks... Do you really have to tell her everything?" he asked the Guide.

"If I don't, I'll cease functioning."

"We've both got it rough, huh?"

The Guide giggled. She flew over to Kuon's ear and whispered, "My owner's just worried. She doesn't want another student going off to die."

"I can hear you!" Kaede said.

The Guide stuck her tongue out. She was definitely passing that Turing test.

"I'll do whatever it takes to turn Kuon-sama into a great Maneuver Cavalleria!" she said, saluting. "Call me your Guide, your familiar, your ghost, whatever you like."

"Do you have a name?"

"No."

"Can I give her one?" he said, glancing at his master.

"Do what you want," she replied.

"A name!" the Guide said, eyes glittering.

"What's your model number?"

"NSR-250R-SE92."

NSR...

"Then I'll call you En."

"En...En..." she said, trying it out. Then En smiled happily. "Thank you so much, Kuon-sama! It's stupidly literal and you clearly have no naming sense at all, but I like it!"

She was definitely his master's Device.

Seven years passed.

Kuon's life was exactly as hellish as he'd wanted.

After starting primary school, he visited the training school three times a week. He usually fell sound asleep in the car on the way home. En supervised his self-training the rest of the week. The first four years were all fundamentals, and he rarely donned the Division Maneuver. Shichisei Kenbu was fundamentally a martial art and he worked on every aspect, from endurance-building runs to body management to swinging a sword until he had calluses. His parents were bemused by the whole thing.

The next three years involved a lot of training in the DM. In the third year, Kuon won the Junior Cup for his Division class in the Jogen Islands DM Combat Championships. To anyone who watched, the difference in skills was clear, but not that many people cared to watch the Division 1 tournament.

But Kuon was satisfied so long as his father, mother, master, and En saw him.

Holding the trophy on the podium, he saw his parents running toward him, far happier about it than he was, and he realized his life goals had changed somewhere along the line. He would kill the Queen; that much hadn't changed. But he would do it so these people could live in peace.

His victory in this tournament was enough to let him enter the famed Cavalleria training school, Jogen Maneuver Academy, even as a Division 1. Nanahoshi Kaede was the headmaster of this school as well as her own, and she planned on training many Cavalleria, every bit as powerful as the Hero had been, before the Jave Queen returned.

Joining their ranks made Kuon feel like he was finally taking the first step on his path to becoming a Maneuver Cavalleria. Though, he was still a bit short of that goal.

But he was ready for it.

It was three days before a talentless no-name would astonish the assembled geniuses at the entrance ceremony.

INTERMISSION: HANABI'S DIARY 1 \\\\\\\

Imperial Era 356. April 5th. Suzuka Hanabi.

The cover to *Portrait of the Hero* fell off. I've lost count of how many times I've read it. I feel like it's my origin story. I want to be as strong as the Hero, to live as he did. Any time I get a long break like this, I find myself thinking about that.

The entrance ceremony is tomorrow. I'll have to find a new member to join our squad, as well as replace the one who graduated. In the meeting, we'll be selecting one of the high school first years. We'll only have a year to watch over them, but we'll make the most of it. I hope we find a good one...

UNOFFICIAL RECORDS

Imperial Air Force: Assault Reconnaissance Unit. Today's MIA Count: 6.

DIVISIONMANEUVER

CHAPTER 2

The Hero Enrolled

IT WAS APRIL. The cherry trees lining each side of the road—fitting for an island with so many capital city evacuees—were in full bloom on the day of the Jogen Maneuver Academy entrance ceremony.

The sole Cavalleria training school on the islands, Jogen Maneuver Academy contained both middle and high schools, and, if you were denied entrance, there was almost no chance of becoming a Maneuver Cavalleria.

The young Cavalleria candidates who made it through the intense selection process—400 applicants to a single successful entrant—could be proud of their accomplishments, and ready to test themselves against their fellow elite.

This year, only one hundred students had been accepted. Ten were Division 4. Eighty-nine were Division 3.

The remaining one wasn't even Division 2. Naturally, this was Okegawa Kuon, Division 1, now thirteen years old.

After the gift of a lecture from the headmaster ("We don't need a Hero who stands above us all. We must all be heroes!"), the new students assembled on the third training ground. Jogen Academy had quite a bit of land. Of the nine training grounds, this was the largest. It was so large that calling it a "ground" seemed like an understatement. It was more of a prairie. Here, they held recreational mock battles between classes. The matches were ten one-on-one fights. If you lost all your matches, you were immediately expelled. Acceptance to the school was no guarantee you could ever become a Cavalleria. The pruning had already begun.

As the new students stood in formation, wearing the Division Maneuvers the school had provided, people began whispering.

"Why is there a talentless Division 1 here?"

"That's beyond embarrassing. It's downright dangerous."

"But he passed the entrance test?"

"I hear he's a relative of the headmaster. This is nepotism."

"Ugh, screw that guy then."

They were, of course, talking about Okegawa Kuon.

He stood out for all the wrong reasons. The frame he wore, Soukyu (Mod), was his personal frame. The Division Maneuvers provided by the school couldn't be piloted by anyone his class. That alone made him stand out, but the fact that he had an AI Device with him was only making it worse. He already had no magic worth using, so why waste any of it on a Guide? Was he an idiot? Was he outright insane? Should they be worried? Kuon could feel the mood gathering around him. Some people were even talking loud enough for him to hear.

Meanwhile, Kuon himself was totally confident. While the DM was operational, En was out of sight, merged with Kuon's Device. Only he could hear her whispering in his ear.

"Heheheh, you're the talk of the school, Kuon-sama."

She didn't sound worried at all—more like she was enjoying it.

"Can't blame them. Long as they don't start throwing rocks."

"Plenty came flying your way when you started primary school. They went real quiet after the first DM class, though. Shrapnel on your left, above."

"Got it. Also, really?"

"You beat up the entire class, remember?"

"Oh, that. Not really fair. I only went through thirty of them. Activate Armament 'Ichi.'"

"You were so much stronger people called you a coward."

"Had that in my last life, too. Not fazed by it now. And I can't lay a finger on Master even when she's not in a DM, so you can't call me strong."

"Again with the modesty. That makes it worse, you know!"

"I mean it. In my last life, I'd already beaten her once by the time I was in junior high, and she was wearing a DM at the time."

"Well, that's fair. You don't have the talent this time, so you'll need a little more mettle to become a Cavalleria."

"Seven years till the Queen returns... No time at all. First step is to get myself on a student squad."

"You can say that again... On your right."

"I see it."

He deployed his Ultra Magic Hardened Blade to protect his

right knee. A moment later, Kuon blocked his opponent's Blade with his own.

"D-damn it!" the Division 3 student yelped, surprised.

"Mm, sorry," Kuon said, and his Blade slipped right in, taking out the DM's Core—its weak point. His opponent's frame ceased all movement, and a fourth star appeared before Kuon's eyes.

They were in the midst of a mock battle. Kuon had just finished his fourth match, easily overpowering opponents with far more raw talent than him. He had chatted with En the entire time.

His fifth opponent was decided swiftly. The next student was a Division 4 in an All-Rounder DM that leaned toward ranged combat.

Kuon moved to the designated block. DM tech had advanced over the last thirteen years; rather than display information on a visor, it was now linked directly to the Cavalleria's magic and displayed in their actual vision. In his field of view were several large cubes that were invisible to the naked eye. These large boxes were the individual match locations.

Kuon's frame, Soukyu (Mod), was a low-spec frame used for practice, and he'd fine-tuned it to his needs. It could only fly for a few minutes, and very slowly at that—it may as well not be able to fly at all. At best, it allowed him to hover just above the ground. It had minimal armaments as well; just a single small, low-powered rifle, and two Ultra Magic Hardened Blades. He'd tuned the thing for combat, combined with his Machine Fencing, but the difference was negligible. It was far worse than the Nichirin, the most common frame used by Division 2s. It was ridiculous to even consider comparing it to the Getsuei (8-Phase) that Suzuka Hachishiki had worn.

But Kuon was winning in his frame.

His opponent was waiting for him. Spiky hair, beady eyes; he seemed like a hot-headed boy. Kuon raised a hand by way of greeting.

"Nice to meet you. I'm Okegawa Kuon. Division 1."

"So, you're the Division 1 everyone's talking about. Wait... four in a row? Are you super lucky or...?"

His opponent clearly couldn't believe the stats they were viewing. "They're all so rude," En whispered in Kuon's ear. He just shook his head.

The Division 4 continued without giving his own name, his tone filled with contempt. "Well, your luck ends here, you talentless boy. You've avoided getting expelled today, but you'll live to regret that. The longer you stay here, the more pathetic you'll feel. Enjoy it while you—"

"Sure sure, but can we get started before someone gets mad? The headmaster can be real scary."

In this school, Headmaster Nanahoshi frequently taught classes herself. Even now, she was personally supervising all the matches. Kuon's intention was simply to warn his opponent about her temper. The spiky-haired boy, however, viewed this as an interruption by an inferior and flew into a rage.

"You'll pay for that, asshole!"

Typical.

Spiky slammed the Standby button. Kuon also reached to the console displayed in mid-air, putting up the indication. Once both were in Standby, a countdown appeared before their eyes.

"I'll crush you," snarled Kuon's opponent.

"I'm telling the truth. She really is scary when she's angry," Kuon said, Blade at the ready.

The count hit zero, and the Division 4's frame shot upward. He aimed his rifle at Kuon, who remained stuck to the ground.

"Division 1, and you think you can shoot your mouth off like that?"

Very few humans had enough magic to be in Division 4. Spiky had been unstoppable in primary school, his vast pool of magic powering a high-output, high-function DM. Kuon's frame was entirely incapable of keeping up with his movements.

So Kuon didn't go after him.

From above, Spiky rained magic bullets down on him. They scattered like shotgun pellets, so each individual bullet wasn't that strong. But if even one scored a direct hit on Kuon's Division 1 frame, it would count as him being unable to continue the match, and he would lose instantly. They were, of course, using mock bullets, but it would still hurt quite a bit if he were hit. Kuon took a deep breath.

Shichisei Kenbu: Tensetsu.

Kuon called upon the Machine Fencing that had made him unbeatable in his past life. Seven years of training with his master had been more than enough for Okegawa Kuon to relearn the Shichisei Kenbu arts.

This was the reason he'd won the Junior Tournament, and how he'd scored four victories in a row at a school for geniuses. Now, the fifth star was right before his eyes.

Tensetsu pushed Kuon's senses through the dimensional barrier. To him, it was as if time had stopped. He found himself in a world where black was white, staring at bullets that didn't move.

Through the rain of bullets that would instantly "kill" him, he saw every route he could follow to avoid them; and not just that. Twelve years of training in his past life, seven in this life, nineteen years in all—this had been enough to hone the core art of Tensetsu to even further heights. Now he could not only see where the attacks were, he could predict where his opponent would go based on the shots they'd taken.

Strangely enough, lines for attacks unleashed at peak form led directly to a foe's weaknesses. Kuon narrowed his opponent's movement down to three options and elected to unleash attacks at all three with his rifle and Blades.

He released Tensetsu. Kuon's frame spun across the ground like it was dancing through the rain of bullets, emerging completely unharmed. As it did, Kuon fired two bullets himself. Both missed, but his main UMH Blade used the momentum from his evasion to pierce his opponent's Core.

"Ungh!" Spiky yelped, feeling a sudden pain in his chest. The direct hit had seemingly come out of nowhere. The Blade was stopped by a barrier right above the Core, and he stared at it in disbelief. As the Blade slowly fell away, his eyes followed it. "What did you just do...?"

Kuon had dodged his shots and thrown a Blade at him. As his opponent stared at nothing, Kuon retrieved his Blade and bowed like a samurai.

"Your aim is swift, but your frame was off balance. I'm off to the next match."

"Huh...?"

By the time Spiky looked up, Kuon was already gone.

Okegawa Kuon was the only person to win nine in a row. At this point, people were beginning to take notice. Two students, waiting for their own matches, were absently gazing at Kuon's.

"Uh, that Division 1..."

"Okegawa Kuon, was it? He's something else."

"What even is that? Fencing...of some kind?"

"I dunno, man. But doesn't seem like aerial combat works against him."

"Yeah, like...wow."

Kuon had just easily one-shot another Division 4.

Both watchers spoke as one.

"He's *good*."

Around them, several other students had their eyes glued to Kuon's block. Those who noticed Kuon's unnatural strength fell into one of two categories, with the first type being too proud and certain of their own elite status to admit his ability was real, so they ignored him.

"*Sigh*... No way those weird tricks would be useful in a real fight. He can't even do basic aerial combat. Letting a Division

1 who can't even fly into a place like this is ridiculous. We're the best the Empire has. Don't let some talentless kid get in our way."

"If you don't have the talent, why bother even trying to fight? All he's done is ruin someone better's chances of getting in here. A waste of the school's resources. What's the point of letting Division 1s think they can be Cavalleria, too?"

"A fluke like that won't last long. No point even watching."

The second type were beginning to admit that, though Kuon may be a Division 1, he was stronger than any of them. They elected to watch him every chance they had.

"He's insanely good! Is he seriously Division 1? Holy crap!"

"I've never seen anyone like him. I thought I knew all the serious Cavalleria candidates, but... Oh, because he's Division 1."

"Whatever the Division, if you're good, you're good. I wanna know why he's so strong. I'll uncover his secret and make it my own!"

"Man, I can't believe anyone like him existed. Watch and learn. He's gonna change how combat's done!"

Watch or don't watch. Consciously or unconsciously, one-third of the new students chose the first option. Fascinatingly, most of those had won six or more battles—they were the ones skilled enough to dominate the mock combat.

They quietly canceled their matches, gathering around Okegawa Kuon's block to watch his final match. What they saw was unbelievable.

For Okegawa Kuon's final match, the student designated as his opponent was the one Cavalleria widely considered the strongest Jogen Maneuver Academy—an elite school with a 0.25 percent acceptance rate—had ever had.

Jogen Maneuver Academy High School Class 3-A, seat number 12, an Attack Gunner in the Lunatic Order Fuji Squad.

Her name: Suzuka Hanabi.

_/////////⌐

Ten minutes prior to her mock battle, Suzuka Hanabi had been in an entirely different training ground from the one the new students were using.

A beautiful girl—or woman—she was built like a model: tall and slim, narrow waist, an athletic build but rather large bust, long black hair tied in a ponytail in the back...

Her looks were perhaps almost too impeccable for her actual age. You could say she was the sort of beauty who looked out of place in a school uniform. If she put on a suit, she'd look more like a teacher than the actual headmaster ever would.

Hanabi was eighteen, famed for being the best Cavalleria in the school's history. Thanks to her good looks and straightforward personality, she was quite popular. People called her the Bushi Hime—the Warrior Princess.

"Hmm..."

Hanabi was watching the first-year high school students' mock battles, scouting them. All of them had survived this school for three years now and had clearly acquired skills beyond simply using their magic to overpower opponents.

None of them are bad, she thought. But neither were they what she was looking for. She'd just watched a Division 3 girl run circles around a Division 4 boy, and in the next block over was a boy whose aerial posture and shot accuracy were quite impressive.

But that wasn't enough. None of them were so good she could invite them to join the Lunatic Order Fuji Squad without reservations.

Suzuka Hanabi was part of the Air Force, officially titled the Imperial Air Force, Lunar Defense Force, First Mobile Unit, Student Echelon, Fuji Squad.

They were called the Lunar Defense Force because they were in charge of defending the Jogen Islands (*Jogen* meaning "crescent moon"), and "Mobile Unit" was a term for any unit composed of Division Maneuver fighters. On top of that, Cavalleria Cadets, students given odd jobs for the experience and sense of accomplishment, were labeled the Student Echelon, which itself was composed of several teams. Hanabi's team was run by a third-year student named Fuji Jindo, and the Fuji Squad was named after him.

That was an extremely long title, so the student squads were usually called Lunatic Order ___ Squad for short.

Not just anyone could join the Lunatic Order. Only a select few students were allowed in. The Fuji Squad currently had three members, including Hanabi. One member had already graduated the previous year. Most squads had four members, so they were looking for another. She was scouting candidates for that position, but not finding any.

The student who'd graduated had been a front-line attacker

like Hanabi. He'd graduated at the top of his class and right into the main forces, so it was pointless comparing them to him. Even so...they were still lacking.

She was looking for a partner. Someone who could fight by her side. Student Echelons may be given mostly odd jobs, but there were times when they went on patrol with groups from the main army. Most of the time, they provided rear support and never even saw an enemy, but it was still real combat. Thanks to the DM, there were rarely any disasters, but you could never be sure what would happen.

A student she could trust to guard her back and her life... She was never trying to find someone *that* good. What she wanted was someone who could at least be counted on to save their own lives. A Cavalleria who could protect themselves. Suzuka Hanabi believed that was what the Lunatic Order needed.

Maybe that girl from earlier...no, it's rude to pick someone if you aren't sure. But...

As she thought in circles, she received a call on her Device. The sender's name displayed on the edge of her magic-linked vision: Motegi Rin, a childhood friend, classmate, and fellow Fuji Squad member. Hanabi looked momentarily relieved, then swiped to accept the call.

"This is—" she began, but was cut off.

"Yo, Hanabi! Not finding anyone good?"

Rin's joyful face filled the window. She wore glasses and looked rather meek, but Hanabi knew better. Rin was much stronger than she looked.

Hanabi glanced around quickly and said, "Why do you think that?"

"Decisive is your middle name! No way you'd take this long otherwise."

"I dunno about that."

"Well, why not go take a look at the new students? Word is one of them's something else."

"The new... You mean the junior high kid? Don't be absurd. We can't recruit a child."

"I took a look at him, and...I think he might actually be better than you."

Hanabi felt the hair on her neck rising.

"Kid gives a new definition to the word *genius*," Rin added.

"You mean that?"

Hanabi trusted Rin's eye for talent. She may spend most of her time goofing off, but she could tell someone's weaknesses at a glance, and almost never offered up praise for anyone. But now she was. And she was saying he was at Hanabi's level?

"Whoa, whoa, don't you start getting heated on me. Keep it cool, okay?"

"I'll try."

But when she waved her hand to end the call, it was a wild swing. She was sure Rin had winced at her for it.

"Right."

Keep it cool. Stay frosty. Just take a look. Just a look.

She turned and headed to see the school's strongest junior high student, walking very quickly. She found it hard to believe.

Even with Rin's word, he was a brand-new junior high school student, just a thirteen-year-old child.

When Hanabi reached the third training ground, she realized her error. She had forgotten to ask his name or even get any sort of description. Even if there was buzz about him, it would be hard locating him among a hundred-odd other students.

She was about to call Rin back when she saw him.

She'd just happened to look right at him. He was dodging a hail of bullets he should have never been able to avoid. Not a single movement was wasted. He then threw a Blade to take out his opponent. He'd taken two shots as well; a feint? The eyes below his short, scruffy hair were beautiful, as sweet as they were gallant. She didn't know this boy, but she felt absolutely certain.

This was him.

That was the moment Hanabi would think back on again and again.

The moment she saw him, her heart leapt. It was like an upward wave rushing through her so fast it made her mind go blank, as if another version of herself was whispering, "At last we meet." For a moment, she felt certain she was born to meet this boy, a sensation so sweet it was almost numbing. She wanted to stand and watch forever, but she also wanted to get closer, to talk to him.

I must face him.

Yes. Closer. Touch him. Blades clashing, bullets firing...

She wanted to fight him with all her power, no holding back, a full-on battle. If she did that, maybe she'd understand something about him.

Like a fever taking hold, her body moved on its own. Before she knew it, she'd opened a direct line to the headmaster, asking her to let her be that boy's final opponent. Never before had she been so joyed over the perks that came with membership in the Lunatic Order. She went straight to the girls' changing room, stripped off her uniform, and changed into the tight-fitting DM plugsuit, her heart racing the whole time. She needed to face him. She needed to talk to him. She needed to fight him.

Now, he stood across the match block from her. She pored over the limited information displayed about him over and over, like it was a love letter. Her heartbeat refused to slow down. It was all she could do to keep her excitement from showing on her face. She wanted to begin right away, but... *Wait, wait just a moment, I have to read this again.*

His name was Okegawa Kuon.

A Division 1 Cavalleria Cadet.

Kuon's first thought was, "Good."

He wasn't sure why, but when the school's strongest Cavalleria suddenly appeared in front of Kuon, he felt relieved. Even though they'd never met before, she seemed familiar.

"Kuon-sama?" Kaede said. "Her name is Suzuka, too. Was she a relative in your former life?"

He frowned. "Could be... I don't know her, though. Suzuka's parents died and he was shipped off to the orphanage, so he never had much contact with his family."

"I see... Then what's with the way she looks at you?"

"Good question."

Headmaster Nanahoshi had given him a brief explanation. Suzuka Hanabi had asked to be his final opponent, Kaede allowed it, and he should go all out, which he was planning on doing anyway.

She was a Division 5.

"Nice to meet you, Okegawa Kuon-kun. My name is Suzuka Hanabi. I'm sorry to spring this on you out of the blue, but let's make it a good fight."

With an oddly happy smile, she activated her Device.

"Reimei, activate."

A brilliant light shot out of her Device, and rice-kernel-sized cubes swirled all around Hanabi's body. Each of them rolled over and, in the blink of an eye, took shape.

There was a reason people "wore" and didn't "ride" Division Maneuvers. Mechanical armor-like coatings covered Hanabi's limbs and body. Within 0.00078 seconds of activation, a barrier was deployed, and her body began floating. Armor covered her back as well, and a backpack covered in thruster nozzles like a fighter plane appeared via unseen connectors.

This was the Division Maneuver—an armored magical weapon that covered the body like armor and tapped into the magic within to allow humans to fly. Their invention had immediately rendered all previous weaponry obsolete.

Suzuka Hanabi's DM had a bright red frame. The backpack was unusually large, and wings extended from the sides of her back, about as wide as she was tall. The gigantic rifle in her right hand was even larger than the one Suzuka Hachishiki had used previously.

Her info appeared on Kuon's vision. En began reading it aloud.

"Frame name: Reimei (Type-3 Artillery). Division 5 All-rounder, leans ranged. Top spec in mobility, defense, and output. Type-3 Artillery refers to the experimental simultaneous deployment of a high-output rifle and Servants, only made possible by Division 5 magic. Definitely the big shot you've been looking for."

Kuon nodded. This was the fastest route to becoming a Cavalleria. Get picked to be in the Lunatic Order, rack up the accomplishments while at this school, graduate, join the Air Force, and team up with everyone else his master had trained to kill the Jave Queen. This was the first hurdle he had to overcome to get there.

He had to beat this Division 5 as a Division 1. He had to be a giant-killer.

He definitely hadn't expected to be facing the school's best already.

"Looking forward to it, Suzuka Hanabi-senpai."

He pressed Standby and drew his Blade.

"My heart is dancing, Okegawa Kuon-kun," Hanabi-senpai said with, for some reason, an incredibly joyous smile.

As he listened to the countdown, Kuon finally realized just how beautiful she was.

The crowd of new students set up a straw poll.

Suzuka Hanabi: 37 votes.

Okegawa Kuon: 2 votes.

The two voting for Kuon had each lost to him. The spiky-haired kid was one of them, throwing him a vote on a "you beat me, you'd better not lose here" basis, but pretending he wasn't. The other was a Division 4 who would likely have been the strongest new student, had he not fallen hard to Kuon's Fencing.

The thirty-seven backing Hanabi were jealous of the fact that a Division 1 had won nine times running; angry at him for being so good despite his Division; panicking (and feeling left behind) because someone their age had been challenged by the school's best; and realistically assuming he didn't have a chance against her. All of them were at least partially motivated by a desire to see him lose.

Would the weakest magic win?

Would the school's best win?

As the crowd waited with breathless silence, one more vote was cast.

Who else would easily hack into an unofficial group chat the new student group had set up, just to cast a vote herself? Their own headmaster, Nanahoshi Kaede. Not just the school's, but humanity's best Maneuver Cavalleria had cast her vote...

_//////////‾

Until the count hit zero, Kuon was pondering his opening gambit.

My frame can't possibly keep up with a Division 5's aerial mobility. She'll probably go for a ranged attack like Spiky did, so if I use that art to get in closer...

The "1" count vanished. As it did, a beautiful face appeared in front of him, smiling.

Huh?

Two Blades swung toward him, one on each side. He only managed to block them out of pure unconscious reflex. The force of them was like being caught in a giant pair of scissors. Her DM's power was overwhelming. Soukyu's arms let out a horrible grinding noise.

Hanabi had gone for a close-up fight.

This, with her giant rifle and range-focused wings?!

Kuon's mind was screaming. Hanabi was so close he could almost feel her breath on him.

"Nicely done, Okegawa Kuon-kun!" she yelled, grinning. "But what's next? I'm clearly overpowering you. You'd better do something before I cut you in half!"

I know!

Kuon momentarily pushed back, then went limp. A moment later Hanabi's Blades slammed into the ground, tangled up in Kuon's. Hanabi's Core was exposed, so he threw a right roundhouse kick at it, but Hanabi recovered her balance instantly and jumped back, out of range.

With their swords locked, Hanabi noticed Kuon putting his strength into it and increased her own to match. When he pulled back a moment later, she hadn't reacted in time.

The first three years after he'd resumed his Shichisei Kenbu training had seen Kuon sans DM, entirely focused on learning sword skills from his master. No longer reliant on overpowering his opponent, between his resolve to do better this time around and the ease with which a child's brain learns, Kuon was now much better at Fencing—and only Fencing—than the Hero Suzuka Hachishiki had ever been.

"Sometimes it's better to yield, huh? Is that the secret to your strength?!"

Even as she dodged backward, Hanabi was smiling. Kuon followed, not about to let her get away so easily.

But...wait, wasn't this too easy?

Shichisei Kenbu: Tensetsu.

The world paused, all colors reversing. Kuon squinted, trying to read his opponent's attack—and right where he would be a second later, he saw a web of enemy attack lines. He didn't have time to wonder what that meant. He could extend his perception of time, but not indefinitely. Just as Tensetsu's effect wore off, his reeling mind finally found the answer...and time moved again.

"Unhhh!"

He hit the brakes, hard. He barely stopped in time. Several thin magical beams appeared, burning the air in front of him, just as he'd foreseen.

"Nicely dodged!"

Hanabi was full of praise. Was this a sign of her confidence? Was she just battle crazy? More importantly, this attack was from a weapon that could fire in all directions from his blind spot, not a weapon a brawler like Hachishiki had ever learned to use.

The wing-like backpack on the rear of the Reimei (Type-3 Artillery) frame split apart. Each piece of the wings launched themselves away, moving independently through the air like birds.

Servants!

Of course she was using Servants. This was a Division 5 frame with an edge to ranged attacks. The ability to fly miniature mobile drones around like missiles, using her magic link to make ranged attacks from any distance or angle—why would she not take advantage of that?

Or maybe by stopping her first attack, he'd forced her to use them. If he didn't make her go all out, there'd be no meaning in victory.

But the exulted confidence rising inside Kuon was quickly dashed.

"You don't think that's all I've got, do you?"

Barely out of his emergency brake, Kuon's frame was assaulted by the swarm of Servants. He hastily turned and began zig-zagging, moving at random as fast as he could. He couldn't see where the attacks were coming from, and with no way to tell where they were aiming, all he could do was rely on hunches and instinct.

Then...

"Dodge *this*," she said.

He turned, activating Tensetsu. Hanabi had her giant Scout Nova Rifle at the ready.

The Type-3 Artillery system, an experimental combination of a high-power rifle and the miniature drones. The Servants would pin an opponent down, allowing the rifle to finish them off—an ideal form for a ranged frame.

He felt his right side grow tense, but...

Shichisei Kenbu: Chijin.

As Tensetsu ended, Kuon's frame vanished. Hanabi's trigger finger stopped just shy of firing, and she found Kuon in her blind spot to her right.

"Shukuchi," Kuon heard Hanabi whisper. *Exactly,* he thought, swinging his Blade at the perfect angle. *Just like teleportation.*

There was no clash of metal. As he struck her, Hanabi twisted her body, sacrificing half her mobility to avoid a loss. As this was a mock battle, the system "detected" that the Blade had sliced Reimei's backpack. Kuon didn't give her a chance to recover. He swung the Blade back the other way, but Hanabi caught that one.

Their Blades locked again, but, where Fencing was concerned, Kuon had already surpassed the Hero.

Their weapons bounced off each other.

"Hahhhhhhhhhhhhhhhhhhh!"

With a yell, Kuon sent his Blades after the school's best. Hanabi's reflexes were good enough that she barely managed to deflect his first attack, but to dodge a slice from any well-trained swordfighter was fundamentally impossible. No such miracle would occur again.

All Hanabi had now was her natural talent.

"If you can get in close, you need not fear attacks from around you" was common sense in DM combat, to the point that it was even written in textbooks. But Suzuka Hanabi's genius defied common sense.

A beam of light shot out from Kuon's blind spot, blocking his supposedly unblockable second attack.

Wha...?!

Kuon couldn't believe his eyes.

It was a sword of light.

The Servants had bound several microfilament magical beams together, forming six different swords that danced around Hanabi. Kuon froze. *That's not possible!* he thought. Servant control should be no more precise than rolling a ball bearing around a carpet, but this young Cavalleria Cadet was moving them like they were part of her own body. Kuon may have been called a Hero in his past life, but, for the first time, he felt fear. When he froze up, seven swords came hurtling toward him.

Shichisei Kenbu: Ryusui!

Ryusui was a combo art, adding a sword draw to Chijin. Kuon moved so quickly it seemed like he'd teleported again and slashed at his opponent as he passed her. Kuon's art sent Hanabi's swords flying and cut off her DM's left arm.

"Ungh!"

But it was Kuon who grunted in pain. He hadn't come out unscathed. That last exchange had left him without a right arm; the suit had detected the hit and rendered it unusable. Once that happened, it wouldn't let him move it at all.

I've used Tensetsu and Chijin too many times. I don't have the concentration left!

The longer this went on, the worse it was for him. She must have known that, too. Before she moved away into ranged combat, he had to get in close again.

Feeling the heat, Kuon turned...and found Hanabi facing him, grinning happily, with new wings deploying Servant Blades. She lunged toward him.

She was still confident enough to fight him up close. That was the only explanation he could think of as it didn't make any sense to him otherwise. But despite what Kuon thought, and in line with what he'd wanted, the match turned into a Blade-centric slugfest.

_/////////⌐

"Who *is* that?"

The only one who noticed anything wrong with Hanabi was her friend, Motegi Rin, who'd come to watch in secret. Hanabi had always been a bit of a berserker and was infamously prone to challenging anyone strong to a match. She frequently wound up disappointed, since her magic was so much stronger than almost everyone else's that she never got to show what she could really do.

But this was *different*.

"Stay calm and fight." Rin had been telling Hanabi that ever since they'd joined the Lunatic Order together three years ago. It had worked, and lately Hanabi had kept her cool through every match. She measured her own ability against her opponents': strengths, weaknesses, skills, flaws, even their preferences, as she fought. For someone who'd once always won by using the power of a Division 5 to overwhelm them, she now used her brain—and the result was that she'd become the best student the school had ever had.

So what was going on now? Who was this?

Who was this girl so excited her face had turned beet red?

Who was this girl grinning through the fight like she was just happy to be there?

Who was this girl doing only close quarters combat in a suit tweaked for ranged combat, just so she could look this boy closely in the face then look embarrassed about it?

"My adorable little Hanabi..." Rin sighed. "You're making me jealous."

But Rin looked awfully happy about it, too.

_//////////⌐

Their match was advancing to the next level.

Kuon had known from the start that the difference in their magic put him at a disadvantage in a long fight, so he kicked things up a notch. He used Tensetsu each time their blades clashed, trying to make each slash a match finisher.

Hanabi sent three Servant Blades at Kuon. He stopped time with Tensetsu, found the lines those swords would follow, and read the trajectories from the other Servant Blades. He found an angle which left her open, predicted how she would dodge, and decided the path of his own Blade and movement.

Time Freeze plus Predicted Future.

An incredible amount of hard work had raised Tensetsu to this level, but, even so, Kuon's Blade couldn't quite reach her.

Time moved again. Kuon dodged all of Hanabi's Blades and swung his sword at her, certain it was too late for her to do anything about it. But her reaction was slightly faster than he expected, and as her Blade blocked the strike, her Servant Blades wheeled around for a counterattack. Kuon immediately used Tensetsu again, plotting a new evasion route and a new attack. This repeated *ad infinitum*.

Both of them were tiring out. Kuon's Time Freezes grew shorter and shorter. When the match had started he could stop time for ten full seconds; but now, it barely lasted three. Since only his consciousness could move, he didn't get a chance to catch his breath. All he could do was move his eyes and his mind, looking for a way to keep himself alive and hopefully deal a fatal blow to his opponent.

Meanwhile, Hanabi was no longer confident.

Using her six Servant Blades with this degree of precision was like threading a needle. It required careful attention and steady nerves. At the same time, she was using everything her physical training could put out to stave off Kuon's intimidating onslaught, and "stave off" was all she could do. She knew for a fact she was attacking from angles he couldn't see, yet none of her attacks hit him. He wove through her four defensive Blades, always attacking from the single angle that was hardest to defend against.

Slice, thrust, cut, swing forward, backslash, strong hit, parry and strike, trip, quick draw, stab, side strike, rain slash, right, left, overhead blow, reverse...

Each blow was precise, every cut good enough to end this. If her responses were even a fraction too slow, she was done for. But Kuon never once even looked like he was dodging Hanabi's attacks. They just never hit him.

As efficient as Kuon's attacks were, he always appeared to just be going from one to the next. It felt like Hanabi's Blades were missing all on their own.

To Hanabi, it was as if Kuon could see the future, and she was half-right about that.

It was like they were dancing. Almost as if they'd taken each other's hands, their steps in sync, supporting one another, swinging each other around, spinning round and round, their sword-play alternately furious and elegant. Each were considering their opponent, guessing how the other would think, act, and react.

In that polished sword dance, their minds began resonating.

This sort of thing often happened during combat between two rival powers—not only in combat, perhaps, but any form of competition. Putting everything they had into it, seeing everything their opponent had to offer, each drawn to the other...

She's enjoying this, Kuon realized. *She's having such a good time she doesn't want to stop.*

He can read my movements, Hanabi thought at the same time. *He's seeing everything I have to offer. Okegawa Kuon... I can't believe he's only thirteen. He seems way older than me.*

She's so beautiful. What a lovely, lonely girl.

How can he be so strong? What could have happened to him to motivate him to this level of strength?

They were speaking with their swords. An old cliché, but it described exactly what was happening.

Senpai, I...

Kuon-kun, I...

Have never enjoyed fighting anyone so much, they finished in unison.

_//////////

Eventually, the balance tipped in Kuon's favor.

He wasn't sure when he noticed. Their fight was too fast and furious to be certain. Kuon never utilized his winning move because Hanabi had chosen to fight close, despite it putting her at a disadvantage. He could also sense her emotions—he couldn't ignore her desire to keep fighting him like this.

But upsetting the balance was an option.

When his magic had nearly run dry, and Kuon was certain the match couldn't continue a moment longer either way, he finally seized the opportunity.

Here I go, senpai.

The color of his aura shifted. When Hanabi sensed it, a flicker of hesitation crossed her face, but she accepted it. She smiled. *Okay. Come at me. Thank you for keeping me company.*

One of Hanabi's Servant Blades flew toward Kuon. He made no attempt to avoid it.

Clang!

He simply cut it down. The answer he'd found was to destroy her weapons.

Hanabi had staved off Kuon's attacks because she had seven Blades. If even one of them was lost, the balance between them would easily crumble.

Kuon's Blade raced toward Hanabi. Hanabi turned all her Blades into attacking Kuon, as if defending any more was point- less. She was ready for defeat, hoping to take him out in the pro- cess, and was satisfied with that outcome.

Then she felt like Kuon had stopped time for a moment. In a soundless world colored like a negative image, Kuon stared back at her. His eyes spoke to her with terrifying intent. *I'm going to win this,* they said.

A chill ran down her spine.

Kuon stopped attacking her. Instead, he swept all six of Hanabi's Blades away at once. By the time she registered the loss of her Servants, his roundhouse kick had hit home and sent her flying.

Why, Hanabi wondered. *Why break my Blades? Why kick me away? Why put me where I could shift this to a ranged battle, where I'd have the...*

Oh. Was that *why?*

"You shouldn't have," she said.

Reimei (Type-3 Artillery) recovered its balance and she reached her right arm behind her, pulling her Scout Nova Rifle to the fore. She aimed as she raised it, Kuon square in her sights.

A Scout Nova Rifle was a weapon that was more powerful the stronger the wielder's magic was. The "Nova" it fired was magic transformed into an ultra-heated beam of light which traveled at light speed. It vaporized anything it touched.

Returning the favor, since I kept coming in close? You're going to let me shoot all I want here at the end then win anyway?

They were the same, she thought, smiling through the scope.

She was done for, Hanabi realized. Doomed. She'd worked it out; she knew what these feelings were.

He came right at me. He showed me everything. And I...

The magic in Hanabi's rifle's energy pack grew. Kuon stood perfectly still in its sights. Hanabi squeezed every last drop of magic she had left into it. This boy had shown her the essence of his Fencing, so she would show him all she was capable of. This was a shot the headmaster had called the Moonbuster and had forbidden her from using—an unparalleled blast from an unparalleled genius.

"Defend yourself!"

It was a full-power attack from a Division 5.

Hanabi's right arm was dead.

Kuon held the Blade in his left hand, standing with one foot forward in a form known as Shitotsu. She was a dozen meters away from him, and his thrust would never reach her. It was even too far for a throw.

His visor sounded an alarm. The enemy had locked onto him with a rifle charged with so much magic En said it could probably blow up the moon. She was a genius in a very different way from his former self that was Suzuka Hachishiki, and she was putting everything she had into this one attack against his current less-than-genius self, Okegawa Kuon.

This was overkill, too much for him. He was delighted by that. He would respond in kind.

Even at this distance, he was sure he could see her smiling.

The light hit.

He saw her line, leading toward her weakness.

Shichisei Kenbu: Shimetsu.

The thrust Kuon unleashed struck Hanabi's magic light bullet.

Something common to all weapons—not just Division Maneuver ones—using magic in place of bullets was the mechanism which reduced human magic to particles. This mechanism wrapped the magic in a force field and converted it to heat energy. This allowed magic—more or less an invisible life force—to be used as a powerful, superheated light beam.

The purpose of Shichisei Kenbu was to allow the ungifted to compensate for the difference in magic levels. Its ultimate arts were all about making magic attacks ineffective.

Shimetsu was an art which used Tensetsu to perceive the core of the light beam's force field. Once perceived, it allowed the user to shatter and scatter the beam, converting it back into its original magic.

Put simply, Shimetsu negated magic bullets.

The light shattered.

Before the remnants could coalesce, Kuon had already poured the last of his magic into a Chijin. He covered a few dozen meters in an instant, ignoring the dizziness, nausea, headache, and circulation backflow caused by the violent loss of magic, and unleashed his final attack.

Hanabi was right in front of him. She clearly had no idea what had happened. She'd never had her rifle shot negated before. Even then, she was responding, her right hand about to move. Kuon saw this and respected it even as he put the full momentum of his lunge into the swing of his Blade. An instant later, Hanabi's DM, Reimei, exploded. The match was done.

Or, Kuon thought it was, at least.

He couldn't even use Tensetsu. He just watched as Hanabi's DM split and moved away as if in slow motion, and, in minimal gear with her body freed, Hanabi used what she'd learned from all of Kuon's attacks to counter them.

Division Purge.

He never imagined she had something like that up her sleeve.

Kuon's respect was elevated to sheer admiration. Hanabi's hand held a small knife hidden in the grip of her rifle, the trajectory of it matching the sideways slash of Kuon's Blade perfectly. This was one of the moves Kuon himself had used earlier.

Parry and strike!

Showing off his repertoire, even in this short match, had come back to haunt him. Pulling off something like this after seeing it once was what made fighting a genius so dangerous.

He couldn't dodge it now. He couldn't even kill the momentum of his own strike.

Kuon had meant to rocket past her, but Hanabi's body blocked his route, and there was nothing he could do to stop her knife from hitting home.

Kuon's Blade pierced Hanabi's heart.

Hanabi's knife pierced Kuon's.

The system detected both strikes and displayed a result across their vision, but the impact of their clash sent both Cavalleria into a tailspin and neither of them were able to read it.

_//////////

Okegawa Kuon told nobody he'd been Suzuka Hachishiki in a previous life. When he was five, his master told him to keep that to himself.

"Huh? Nobody's gonna believe that, nitwit. They'll think you're a weirdo or straight-up delusional."

A devastating blow.

"And imagine if the Hero did show up again. The idiots in the army would just train him again, send him off to fight alone, and he'd die for nothing, *again*."

The finisher:

"And the way you are, you won't get his results. You're Division 1. You come forward like that, you'll just raise expectations you can't ever hope to meet. You'll be nothing but a big fat liar."

For all these reasons, Nanahoshi Kaede had forbidden

Okegawa Kuon from telling anyone he was Suzuka Hachishiki reborn. If he ever did, not only would she never teach him Shichisei Kenbu again, she'd use every power she had as headmaster to ensure Kuon never became a Cavalleria.

"Indulge that vanity, if you like. Throw your whole second life away. See if I care."

She clearly meant it. From that point on, Kuon didn't even tell his parents he'd been the Hero in his previous life. It was for the best. Like his master said, he no longer had Hachishiki's talent. His experience in his past life had given him some strength, but he couldn't fight like the Hero did. He had to change. Okegawa Kuon had to become strong despite his weakness.

En had also told Kuon something about Kaede in confidence and was severely punished for it later.

"She was absolutely furious with the world and the army for putting everything on the Hero's shoulders and driving him to his death," she'd said, "and with Hachishiki-sama for failing to value his own life. But what she finds hardest to forgive was her own inability to prevent it."

_//////////⌐

Nanahoshi Kaede had put in the sole vote for "tie" and walked off with the betting pool.

Kuon found himself lying on his back on the ground wearing just his plugsuit, his frame gone. He couldn't move. Before he could even wonder *why* he couldn't move, he took a handful of the strangely soft, warm, nice-smelling marshmallow-like thing pressed against his face, and squeezed.

"Eeep!" The marshmallows squealed.

Wait, were these...?

"Are boobs still new to you...?"

Oh, right.

Hanabi was laying on top of him, clad only in her plugsuit, just as he was.

The watermelon-like marshmallows pulled away from Kuon's face. He wasn't sure whether watermelons or marshmallows were a more apt description. His head was spinning. Maybe neither made sense, but the softness had been pleasant. He wanted to savor it a little more...

"Not enough for you?"

"No!" he blurted out before his brain could stop him. Hanabi giggled, still astride him. He had to do something about this reflexive honesty.

"Well done, honest Okegawa Kuon-kun," Hanabi said, her voice wafting down like a gentle feather. Her plugsuit certainly left nothing to the imagination. Her breasts were insanely huge, her waist impossibly thin, yet her backside more than ample. Having a body like that on display was enough to bewitch anyone.

"Same to you, senpai... Um, sorry I let that slip."

"I don't mind. There's no one else here. Nobody else heard you."

"Er... Wh-where are we...?" He looked around. Definitely no one else there.

"The edge of the training ground. We got thrown pretty far. Does it hurt anywhere?"

"No. I used up all my magic and won't be moving anytime soon, but the DM kept me uninjured. So, um, senpai, if you could get..."

He wasn't able to finish that sentence.

Hanabi's face was suddenly inches from him. She stared into his eyes, so close he could feel her breath on his face. Those bountiful breasts rested on top of him, their shape yielding to his chest. Hooray for plugsuits.

"Uhhhhhh, y—"

"You're fascinating."

"Eeep?!"

Kuon's reactions were very suspect.

Unfortunately, at no point in the thirty years he'd lived across two lives had he had any experience with love. His entire life had been spent killing Jave. His soul was currently completely under her spell.

"F-fascinating? I-I don't know how to...heh heh..."

"Where did you learn to use a sword like that? No, I know. That's Machine Fencing. You learned from the headmaster?"

"W-well, I spent some time learning that, I guess..."

"Don't be modest. You must have worked quite hard. You're terrifyingly good. Your skill commands respect."

"M-man, you sure know how to make a guy blush... I don't know if we're talking about the same thing here, though," Kuon said, even though he knew she was only interested in the Shichisei

Kenbu. "You're right," he admitted. "My master is Nanahoshi Kaede."

"I knew it! I've been begging her to teach me, but she never would!"

"Really?"

"She said those arts weren't for outsiders!"

"Umm...she takes students all the time."

"She does?! Argh... Why?! When?!"

"I mean, they all quit in the first couple of months," Kuon said.

"Oh? Why is that?" Hanabi tilted her head, baffled. It was super cute.

"Master always starts with swinging wooden swords and endurance running. She won't let you touch a DM. That's not what those students are looking for, so they all give up."

"I see!" Hanabi nodded. "So your moves are all extensions of normal Machine Fencing." She sat up. She was still on top of Kuon, and her backside was pressing into his belly. Naturally, nobody wore underwear under a plugsuit, so Kuon's abs were getting a very detailed feel of Hanabi's butt. She definitely had childbearing hips.

"Senpai, um!"

"But why? Why won't she teach me? Does she not like me?"

She suddenly looked depressed, so Kuon hastily reassured her. "N-no! I think it's just because you're already strong. You're Division 5!"

"Hm? What's that got to do with it?" Hanabi tilted her head, baffled again. It was even cuter the second time.

"Um...the Hero was one of Master's pupils, but the way he ended up... She feels responsible, apparently. Shichisei Kenbu was originally designed for people who weren't gifted, so she thinks teaching it to a Division 5 led to him getting reckless."

"Reckless..."

"The Hero was kicked out before he learned the ultimate art. But that was because he was always the type to charge in without—"

"Oh, I see. But Kuon-kun, don't forget," Hanabi interrupted, slamming her hands to the ground on both sides of his head. There was a burning rage in her eyes. "We're only alive today because of him. We survive to fight because of the Hero."

"Um...yes...sorry..." He had no idea what Hanabi was mad about, so he just apologized.

"And you're learning this Shichisei Kenbu from the headmaster?" Hanabi asked, her anger gone. She sat up again, still on Kuon's stomach. Quite the posture. When he looked up at her, half his field of vision was filled with jiggling boobs. *Mind elsewhere!*

"Uh, yes..."

"So, you can teach me?"

"Uh...no, I don't... She might get mad..."

"Please, Kuon-kun! Shichisei Kenbu! The Hero learned it! His strength! Teach it to me! I'll do anything!"

She slapped her hands on the ground again. *This... This is a full-screen super beauty plea attack!* he thought wildly. *Think of something else! Anything!* Begging any healthy thirteen-year-old boy like that would make all sorts of images float into his—

"What are you looking at?" Hanabi demanded.

"Your boobs," Kuon answered automatically, unable to lie in the spur of the moment. Hanabi turned bright red and covered her chest with her hands.

"Y-y-you really are! Not once but twice...?"

"Augh, no, no, I wasn't looking, I wasn't! I'm sorry!"

Hanabi turned her head, sulking. Her hands stayed where they were. So cute. "Um, so why aren't you getting off...?"

"Honestly? Thanks to our mock battle, I don't have the strength to stand," she said.

"Huh?! Why didn't you say so?"

"Eeep! No, Kuon-kun, don't move! My legs are quivering! Augh!"

"No, wait, whaaat?"

"What the *hell* are you two doing?"

Kuon froze instantly. His master was staring down at him. Apparently she'd come looking for them after they'd been blown away and failed to respond or return.

"Oh my, Headmaster! I do apologize. We're both out of magic and couldn't get in touch."

Hanabi sure recovered quickly.

I wish I could do that...

Kuon was sure it would just get him a lecture later. His gaze shifted past Hanabi to the blue skies above.

"Oh, I forgot to mention, Kuon-kun."

Kuon and Hanabi's magic had recovered enough for them to activate their DMs and return to the training ground entrance. A pack of new students surrounded them, desperate to hear about the draw between the school's best Cavalleria and Kuon (though they all assumed she'd gone easy on him). They spent a few minutes answering questions before Hanabi spoke to Kuon again.

"I'd like to scout you to my squad—the Lunatic Order Fuji Squad."

...

"Whaaaaaaaaat?!" the crowd erupted.

As the students around them shrieked and yelped, En appeared, looking happy. "Nicely done, Kuon-sama," she said.

And that was how Okegawa Kuon's school life had begun.

INTERMISSION: HANABI'S DIARY 2 \\\\\\

Imperial Era 356. April 8th. Suzuka Hanabi.

I scouted a promising boy during the new student mock battles. He's a first year in junior high. Fuji-kun will probably be against it, but I'm sure he'll come around once he sees what the boy can do.

I'm really looking forward to it. Just thinking about how I can talk to him every day is making my heart race.

Not like that, though!

UNOFFICIAL RECORDS

Imperial Air Force: Assault Reconnaissance Unit. Today's MIA Count: 9.

CHAPTER 3 The Hero Enlisted

IT HAD BEEN THREE DAYS since the entrance ceremony. Okegawa Kuon was put in class 1-A, reserved for the twenty students with the best results in the mock battles. With En in tow, Kuon set foot in that class for the first time.

"G-good morning..."

With his magic completely drained, he'd been unable to move, and was given permission to rest for two days—quite an awkward way to start school. His hesitant greeting immediately silenced the class. Everyone turned to look and froze in their tracks.

For a moment, he was worried. *Did I make myself a target?* he wondered. But then...

"Okegawa!" "Okegawa Kuon!" "Okegawa-kun!" "Okegawa!" "Kuon-kun!" "That guy?" "The Division 1!" "The one who tied with Suzuka Hanabi-senpai!" "He was scouted into the Lunatic Order!" "Smaller than I imagined." "Cuter than I imagined!" "Is that Device a Guide?" "Yo, Okegawa, you're amazing!" "How'd you do that?" "What *was* that?" "You gotta teach us!" "Machine Fencing?" "Is it true you're the headmaster's pupil?" "Is that why you're so good?" "Are you really Division 1?" "You joined the Lunatic Order already?" "The Fuji Squad is so cool!"

He was surrounded and aggressively questioned. Kuon was on the small side and was unable to free himself from the circle. He wound up nervously answering as best he could.

"I'm really Division 1." "I haven't officially joined the Lunatic Order yet." "Yeah, her name's En." "Yes, Machine Fencing." "The headmaster is my master and she's scary." "If I try teaching anyone else Master will get angry, sorry, she's scary." "Look, she's really scary."

When the bell rang and the teacher had come in, Kuon was finally released. The teacher informed him that his seat was in the front row by the windows. She was a sweet-looking young woman by the name of Kadono.

"Okegawa-kun," she began asking, "is it true you're the headmaster's pupil?"

"Yes. She's scary."

After homeroom, classes began. Jogen Maneuver Academy might be a Cavalleria military training school, but they also covered the usual subjects. Nearly all of these included a bias toward how they could be practically applied to combat, however.

There was a display set on his desk, and when he tapped the screen it opened an electronic textbook titled *New Math 1*. He skimmed it. The first chapter was titled "Positive Numbers and Negative Numbers," and the former Hero smiled fondly, reminded of his first twenty-two years of life.

Everything after that was a mad rush.

Everyone wanted to see the Division 1 who'd been scouted to the Lunatic Order on the first day of school. Upperclassmen from the junior high, and even a few students from the high school, swung by to gawk at him.

One day, he was called out by a senpai. His classmates all went pale. The nature of the school made it home to many violent types, as well as many students who took camaraderie quite seriously. Several classmates offered to accompany him, which he appreciated but politely declined. He went alone to the designated location outside the auditorium. *Seems like a crowded location for a fight,* he thought.

He found four tough-looking male students from the high school waiting for him.

"Will you join my squad?!" "No, join ours!" "We asked first!" "No, wait!"

There were eight squads in the Lunatic Order; four of them were trying to recruit him at once.

Hanabi had been right. She warned him people would begin fighting over him, so he should be careful not to accept any offers. She ignored the fact that she'd given him one herself.

"I've already been asked to join the Fuji Squad..." Kuon said, feeling very small around these four.

They simply begged him to at least think about it, growing very insistent, until, suddenly, a beautiful girl swooped in to save him. She pried the poor child away from the coarse men, hugging Kuon's face tightly between her large breasts. "Never!" she said. "He's mine! I won't let anyone have him!"

That touching moment sent a shockwave running through the crowd around them.

The Warrior Princess had gone full dere.

From that day forth, the phrase "Warrior-dere" could be heard in all corners of the school...referring, of course, to Suzuka Hanabi.

Before starting school, Kuon had just been hoping to get into the Lunatic Order somehow. He even worried about whether any squads would be willing to consider a Division 1 like him. It never occurred to him he'd be in such high demand.

It was all thanks to Suzuka Hanabi.

That alone was enough reason to accept her offer, but even beyond that was how much he enjoyed their mock battle. The idea of fighting alongside her excited Kuon. He'd never felt anything like that in his previous life.

So Okegawa Kuon resolved to join the Fuji Squad.

He wasn't trying to make up for having accidentally contributed to the creation of a weird buzzword like "Warrior-dere," nor was he just there because of her boobs. Definitely not!

It never occurred to him Hanabi may not have talked to the Squad Leader about it.

In one corner of the school grounds was a building called the Order Hall. It was an old, three-story building, and one of its rooms was the Lunatic Order Fuji Squad's meeting room.

It was about half the size of a classroom, with a big desk plopped to one side. The entire desk was covered in a large screen, which could produce holographic projections to help briefings and meetings proceed more efficiently.

Currently, it was displaying Kuon and Hanabi's mock battle.

Surrounding the display were chairs, stationery supplies, coffee, snacks, and four people.

A boy Kuon hadn't recognized was the squad's leader, a third-year high school student named Fuji Jindo. He was a handsome boy who gave the impression of being incredibly mild-mannered. Next to him stood Hanabi's friend, Motegi Rin.

Facing them was Suzuka Hanabi, who stood behind Okegawa Kuon with her hands on his shoulders, nodding confidently. "So, this is Okegawa Kuon-kun, the Fuji Squad's newest member."

"W-wait a minute, Suzuka-kun! He's still in junior high! We can't let him—"

"He fought me to a draw. What problem could there possibly be?"

"Well...he's too young. No matter how you—"

"Haha! That's ridiculous. Fuji-kun, you know perfectly well you're always the first to complain about being underestimated by the real soldiers because we're only students. You always say to judge people by ability, not age."

"That's...true, but..."

"And you can always just go up against him in a mock battle yourself."

"No, based on the video... Honestly, it would be no contest at all."

"What's that supposed to mean?"

"You know. I have no way of stopping an attack with his strength behind it."

"So..."

"But that's not the issue. However strong he may be one-on-one, we can't recruit someone who can't work as part of a team. Just like the headmaster always says, we don't need any Suzuka-Hachishiki-style lone heroes. The Hero may have always worked alone, but that isn't what we're looking for. And, just to be clear, I'm not saying this to criticize the Hero."

"I know."

"So don't glare at me like that."

"I'm not glaring!"

The second Hachishiki's name was mentioned, the mood in the room had grown prickly. Kuon wondered why.

"Hanabi's a big fan of the Hero," Rin whispered. "She really looks up to him, so she tends to take it personally."

"I'm not angry!" Hanabi fumed.

"Yeah, yeah, sure you aren't. You aren't angry at all."

Fuji cleared his throat and got the conversation back on track. "Point is, he's only just entered junior high, so he's got no experience with teamwork at all."

"They're starting basic training next week," Hanabi said. "As long as we instruct him alongside that..."

"That's a lot of extra work."

"And it'll be worth it. You've seen what he can do. I've searched the whole school for an attacker who can fight alongside me, and he's the only one there is. If we keep putting it off, another Squad will grab him."

Fuji sighed and gave Hanabi a baleful look. "Suzuka-kun, you know perfectly well that if he joins our squad, he'll be put in real combat at some point. He's a thirteen-year-old child! Is that really a good idea?"

It seemed that was Fuji's biggest concern. Certainly, Okegawa Kuon was physically only thirteen. While the state of the war was much less dire than it used to be, anyone enrolling in a military school knew what that meant—and their parents did, too. Despite that, the very fact that Fuji was reluctant to send a child into real combat made him more a hero than Suzuka Hachishiki ever was.

"W-well..." Hanabi stammered. She glanced at Kuon.

The first image that popped into Kuon's mind when he heard "real combat" was what he'd seen in his last life shortly before his death: the sight of the evacuation flights being shot down one after another, packs of Jave swarming them in mid-air, forcing their way inside. They chewed their way through the citizens trapped within before the planes exploded, leaving only scrap metal, balls of fire, and a rain of human body parts behind. The spectacle had burned into Hachishiki's eyes through his DM's visor.

His body was shaking, and not with fear, but fury.

"Fuji-senpai."

Suzuka Hachishiki's father and mother, the family he'd grown up with in the orphanage... They'd all died like that.

So Okegawa Kuon...

"I want to wipe the Jave out to protect my family. I want to be a Cavalleria so no one I care about dies, and no more lives end eaten by monsters."

This time, I'll kill the revived Queen with my own hands.

Faced with this intensity, Fuji swallowed.

Kuon met his gaze. "If I'm going to do that, I need all the experience I can get. Please. Let me join the Fuji Squad!"

Rin let out a little breath, impressed. Hanabi folded her arms, looking proud.

"See? That's my Kuon-kun! He's great, right? Right?"

"He's not yours, Hanabi."

"Sh-shut up! That's just a turn of phrase!"

"But what do you say, Squad Leader?"

"Hmm..."

"Please!" Kuon said again, bowing his head.

Fuji hemmed and hawed for a moment. "All right," he finally said. "If you're prepared for the consequences, I've got nothing further to say." He smiled and held out his hand. "Welcome to the squad, Okegawa Kuon-kun."

Kuon and Hanabi's faces both lit up. Kuon took Fuji's hand, and Hanabi put both her hands over theirs.

"Thank you!"

"Thank you, Fuji-kun!"

Rin just smiled. "Happy now, Hanabi?"

Fuji released Kuon's hand, but Hanabi kept hers clasped firmly around Kuon's, refusing to let go. "Um, senpai...?"

He turned to find Hanabi's face very close to his, smiling widely. "We have so much to do together, Kuon-kun! I'll teach you everything you need to know!"

"O-okay... Thanks, I guess...?"

Rin's smile grew even broader. "Interesting, Hanabi. I smell a crime in the making here."

Squad Leader Fuji clapped his hands. "With that settled, let's get this meeting started. We need to decide on positions and the training schedule."

A calendar appeared on the screen, showing the proposed schedule. The window next to it was a formal list showing the roster of the Imperial Air Force, Lunar Defense Force, First Mobile Unit, Student Echelon, Fuji Squad.

Squad Leader: Control, Fuji Jindo (Div4). Frame: Tensei (Mindweb).

Subleader: Snipe Gunner, Motegi Rin (Div4). Frame: Yousen (Falcon).

Member: Attack Gunner, Suzuka Hanabi (Div5). Frame: Reimei (Type-3 Artillery).

To the end of the list, Fuji added:

New Member: Front Attacker Candidate, Okegawa Kuon (Div1). Frame: Soukyu (Mod). Undergoing evaluation.

_//////////⌐

At Jogen Maneuver Academy, there were morning classes on Saturdays.

On the way home after school, Hanabi and Rin were walking together in a crowd of excited students, when they saw a familiar—and smaller—figure ahead of them. Rin called out to him.

"Heeey! Kyuu-kuuun!"

Kuon turned around with a pleasant smile, one Hanabi always thought was much too calm for a thirteen-year-old.

"Done for the day, Hanabi-senpai, Rin-senpai?"

"Yep. You, too?"

"Kyuu-kun, heading home?"

"Yes. Lunch with my family, then afternoon practice."

"Oh," Rin said, clapping her hands. "You live close by, Kyuu-kun?"

"Yes. My parents moved so I could attend school here."

"Wow," the girls said in unison.

"So I've gotta do all I can to become a Cavalleria."

"True! You're such a go-getter!" Rin said, mussing up Kuon's hair.

Hanabi gave Rin a look like she couldn't believe the nerve.

"U-um, yeah, keep it up," she said, and mussed Kuon's hair herself.

Rin's glasses gave off a sinister flash, and she let Hanabi take over. As she took her hand away from Kuon's head, she used her Device to take dozens of shots of the nervous smile on Hanabi's face. She was always taking photos of Hanabi, her prized collection all saved to her "Hanabi" folder. She would send the best shots to Hanabi later.

"You both live in the student dorm?" Kuon asked, enduring Hanabi's mussing.

"Yes, it's right behind the school. We're going shopping together today."

"Also, Hanabi and I are roommates. Jealous?"

"Ah...ahaha..."

"Wanna come up and see our room?"

Hanabi was practically foaming at the mouth. "H-he can't, Rin! It's the girls' dorm!"

"Who cares about the 'no boys' rule! Hey, did you know, Kyuu-kun? Hanabi may not look it, but she's a total slob, just drops her clothes wherever. The whole room's filled with girly little shorts and bras you could use to carry watermelons."

"Doooooon't make things up! Never trust a word she says, Kuon-kun! I fold my clothes when I take them off, and my bras aren't *that* big, and my panties aren't that cute or... What are you making me say?!"

"Sad but true, Kyuu-kun. All she wears are the drabbest things. You tell her, too. She really should pay more attention to her underwear or she'll be left high and dry when the moment comes."

"Argh! Can we not talk about my underwear?!"

"By the way, Hanabi?" Rin asked.

"What?"

"How long are you gonna pet Kyuu-kun?"

"..."

"..."

"Ah...ahaha..." Kuon laughed nervously, at a loss about what to say or do. But the way Hanabi yanked her hand away at the speed of light and turned bright red, looking like she was about to burst into tears... That was definitely, really cute.

"Still, Machine Fencing practice? I'm jealous," Hanabi said, feeling much better after delivering a brutal chop to the back of Rin's head.

"Oh, I did ask Master," Kuon said. "She said she wouldn't mind as long it was only the core Fencing techniques. So, if you're okay with me teaching you..."

"R-really?! Th-then you'd be teaching me yourself?"

"Er, yes, if that's okay..."

"Y-you mean...just the two of us...?"

"Y-yes..." Kuon nodded, unsure why Hanabi had suddenly grown so fidgety.

"I... I'd love that."

"Uh...okay then."

There was a long silence.

"..."

"..."

"Hellooo?" Rin interrupted.

"Ah!" Hanabi exclaimed. "How long have you been there, Rin?"

"The whole time. Since this conversation started."

"You really shouldn't sneak up on people like that. Honestly!"

"I didn't..."

"You two sure get along well," Kuon said, shaking his head.

Rin grinned, throwing her arms around Hanabi. "We do! We've been besties since we were little! Right, Hanabi?"

"Get off me!"

"Nooope!"

"I said. Get. Off."

"Ahaha, childhood friends, then? I'm a little jealous. I've done nothing but train since I was little, so I haven't really had any friends."

"What about your Guide-chan?"

"Oh, En? She's more like a watchdog..."

"You called, Kuon-sama?"

A fairy in a suit appeared, accompanied by an inexplicable smoke effect. Even more inexplicable were the cushion she was sitting on, a tea table with an antique, square CRT TV sitting on it next to a basket of tangerines, and the fact that the TV screen was showing the samurai drama, "Kenjutsu Shobai."

"All she ever does is watch reruns, so we don't really have much to talk about."

En gasped. "How could you, Kuon-sama? I am attempting to understand the martial arts my own way, in the hopes of being more useful to you!"

"Who's your favorite actor?"

"Watanabe Atsuro. The first Daigoro was so lovely..." She began drooling.

"Who?" Hanabi and Rin asked at the same time.

"See? She's weird like that. Still, she's probably the closest thing to a friend I've had, so...so... Wow, I really want to cry right now."

"You're so mean, Kuon-sama!" En pouted.

Rin laughed. "You seem pretty close."

"Not at all."

"You're so *mean*, Kuon-sama!"

"Oh, but..." Kuon added, "I've made a lot of friends in my new class, which is great! It's good to have people working toward the same thing you are." He gave a smile that was every bit the smile of a child his physical age. "And we haven't gone into combat yet, so none of them have died!"

But no, he definitely doesn't seem like a child his age at all, Hanabi thought.

"Kyuu-kun, you—" Rin began, her smile vanishing.

Hanabi cut her off, smiling. "Right, you have us now! We might be a little older, but we're all in the Lunatic Order together. Let's help each other out! If you ever need anything, you can rely on your squad!"

"I will!" Kuon said, enthusiastically.

Hanabi glanced at Rin, giving her a slight nod as if to say, *No worries*.

Rin sighed and let it be. If Hanabi said it was good, then it was.

Hanabi rubbed Kuon's head again.

By the following Monday, "undergoing evaluation" was no longer listed after Okegawa Kuon's name on the Fuji Squad roster. Kuon had officially become part of the Lunatic Order.

There were eight Lunatic Order squads, and they were all ranked according to their achievements and battle results. The higher your rank, the more likely you were to be taken into combat zones, and the school's engineers would prioritize tune-ups on your frames. The Fuji Squad was currently ranked second.

Mock battles between the squads—a big factor in the ranks— were held three times a week. Today, the day after Kuon officially became part of the Fuji Squad, was the first battle.

At the entrance to the training ground practice block, Fuji said, "Let me go over the positions again, Okegawa-kun.

"You're the Front Attacker, so you're on the front lines. Your job is to cut your way into the enemy squad. Some people tank it, but I'd prefer you go wild, taking full advantage of your hand-to-hand and flanking skills.

"Suzuka-kun is the Attack Gunner, so she'll be with you at the fore. But she'll be mixing it up with mid-range attacks. In our squad, she'll either support your efforts, slicing into the enemy with you, or drop back and cover you from a distance.

"Motegi-kun is the Sniper Gunner, so she'll stay at the rear. She uses precision long-range shots to diminish the enemy forces. She'll also help create openings for the two of you to break through their line.

"My role is Control—I give instructions to the squad. Different Cavalleria handle the role in different ways. Some stay close to the front line and help break through, while others remain at the rear sniping with the gunners. I tend to stay in the middle, providing support to both fore and rear lines as needed.

"And that's the gist of it. Any questions...? Good, then let's get started."

Kuon, Hanabi, and Rin all nodded. Everyone activated their Division Maneuvers. "Getting thrown right in the thick of it, huh," Kuon muttered, not feeling that confident. Even when he was Hachishiki, he'd done almost no team exercises.

"I'll issue the orders. You simply focus on getting yourself in range of the enemy."

"And then?"

"Well, that's your specialty, isn't it?"

Cut them down, eh?

"Everyone ready? If we win today, we'll be ranked first. Let's do this!"

Fuji pressed Standby for the team as a whole. The countdown began, then reached zero.

Kuon nervously tried making his brain focus on what he had to do. *So...Front Attacker. Cut into them. Victory condition is to take out all enemies or shoot down the Control. If we run out of time, the team with the most survivors lives. So first, I gotta get in close.*

The block set up for the team matches was four times the size of the one from the opening ceremony's individual matches. They began at opposite corners, and it would be several seconds before they could engage. Teams would use that time to take up positions, getting all their members into advantageous positions. Logistics were the key to war, information the key to strategy, and positioning the key to combat.

Kuon completely ignored positioning. He'd forgotten it a long time ago.

"Okega—"

"Kuon-kun!" Hanabi's yell interrupted Fuji's.

By the time their cries reached his ears through the DM's comms, the enemy beams were almost on him. Of all things, the former Hero had run directly toward the enemy squad. Even a Division 5 would have a tough time surviving a barrage like that.

One unit down already. Everyone on both teams assumed as much. But...

Shichisei Kenbu: Tensetsu.

Like always, the Division 1 stopped time and slipped through the storm of beams. He hadn't survived so many battles with monsters from another world for nothing. But Kuon had forgotten one thing: He was fighting humans today.

He released Tensetsu.

An instant later, there was a *fwip*.

"Huh...?"

A pain ran across his chest. A mock bullet had hit him. The DM detected he'd been shot down.

"Oh, a sniper, Kuon-sama," En said, clearly enjoying this. "I guess mankind is better at sniping than the Jave. Even a hero falls quite easily. Good, good."

He put En's peals of laughter on mute, wishing he could turn invisible. He glanced at the image of his senpai in the corner of his vision.

"Sorry..." he muttered.

They all smiled awkwardly, then Hanabi went and won the match for them.

"No, you're not to blame. That was my oversight. I should have mentioned the opening volley would include delayed shots. Sorry."

Fuji seemed totally serious. Making a beeline toward the enemy was completely stupid, but Fuji avoided pointing out the obvious. He was clearly a good leader.

Kuon was still dragging around some bad habits from his previous life. He'd spent thirteen years in this one already, but only began wearing a DM in earnest four years ago. A reckless streak had been with him through the individual matches, but now it was becoming painfully obvious.

"Time for training," Fuji grinned. His eyes, however, were *not* smiling.

Kuon felt like this senpai might be every bit as bad as his master, but all he could do was bow his head and agree.

Even ordinary classes were all about mock team battles.

Middle class 1-A drew lots and were split into teams of four then pitted against each other. The only victory bonus here was the achievement.

On weekdays, Kuon had Lunatic Order missions or training after class. Saturdays were Shichisei Kenbu training with his master. Thanks to this relentless schedule, Kuon's movements in team exercises improved quickly.

He would approach from the side so as to not interfere with the gunner's opening barrage, cutting into the enemy formation with the other frontline units on his team. Faced with the only junior high first year in the Lunatic Order, along with a Front Attacker from the school's strongest team, enemies mainly took one of two strategies: try not to let him get close, or face him head on.

Neither worked out well for them. Kuon was unstoppable.

New students weren't great snipers, but his team's Sniper Gunners silenced the enemy gunners from a distance anyway, giving time for the two frontline attackers to slice through the enemy. If they were in front of him, he could evade their sniping, take out the gunner or their Control, and secure victory.

He wasn't just better; he was unbeatable.

This was more or less to be expected. The only Cavalleria here who stood a chance against him were Hanabi and Headmaster Nanahoshi. It only took a few battles for his classmates to figure that out and begin grumbling.

"If you get on the same team as Okegawa, you're always gonna win."

"And if you're not on Okegawa's team, you're definitely gonna lose."

"Our results are entirely at the whim of the lots..."

"What's the point? I mean, why are we even here?"

Geniuses who'd survived the 0.25 percent cut-off were losing confidence left and right.

"This is hardly worth calling practice!" Kadano said. She was both their homeroom teacher and the DM instructor. "Okegawa-kun, no more Attacker roles. You aren't allowed to attack at all. You take the Control role."

That was quite a stiff demand. But Kuon had been taking orders from Fuji for a while now. It shouldn't be too hard to do the same with Kadano.

It was.

Kuon's instructions were so completely off base that his team was plunged into the crucible of confusion.

He was fine during the opening barrage. He had sent two attackers around the sides of it, which was fine; routine stuff. After that, it was a disaster. He thought the enemy weren't shooting much, and a moment later two of his team were surrounded by three of theirs and beaten to crap and back. He only realized the enemy were suspending the barrage early and laying ambushes for his attackers after his teammates had pointed it out after losing the same way three times in a row.

The next time, he sent a gunner forward alongside the attackers. They were all wiped out by the opening barrage. The looks his teammates gave him were murderous.

"Okegawaaa..." they said angrily.

"S-sorry..."

Once Kuon began losing, he grew less aggressive. Even once the barrage ended, he'd sit still, waiting for the enemy to come attack. The enemy sent attackers in one at a time. While he had his team dealing with them, he found the enemy Control standing behind him with a gun to his head. He'd been so focused on the enemy in front of him that he hadn't noticed the Control at all and was swiftly taken out.

With Kuon in Control, his teams never won once.

"Don't worry about it. I mean, even you have things you can't do."

"It's kind of a relief."

"Seriously! Okegawa's only human!"

His classmates tried cheering him up, but that was a depressing day. When he went to the Fuji Team meeting room after school, Hanabi saw how dejected he looked, asked why, then said, "Time for training."

They went through the Fuji Squad's Control records. Hanabi seemed delighted to sit next to Kuon and explain things. Kuon asked her everything he didn't understand, and every time she puffed up her oversized chest, laying her interpretation on him. He made sure to take detailed notes. Her boobs were still big. So very big. And jiggly.

The next day was a Lunatic Order rank match.

Kuon paid close attention to Fuji's orders, and he was shocked by how quickly decisions were made. Fuji never once hesitated. These squads knew each other's tactics and abilities like the backs of their own hands with tactics shifting between frontal assaults and attempts to catch each other off guard at dizzying speeds. No matter what happened, Fuji gave clear instructions that led them to victory, and Kuon was extremely impressed.

It wasn't just Fuji; Hanabi, the school's strongest Cavalleria, could slice into enemy lines or lay down support fire with a skill that made even the former Hero's eyes widen. As for Rin, her sniping was terrifying. One second she'd be laying down a barrage to blind her opponents, and the next a single precision shot would cut right through all of that. It was a trick one could only pull off by switching between two types of rifle in less than a second. Kuon frequently wondered if Rin actually had four arms.

The following were the highlights of the match that impressed Kuon the most:

After the standard opening barrage, Hanabi and Rin continued relentless gunfire. Unable to ignore not only the support fire from the Control and the Snipe Gunner's sniping, but also the Division 5 Scout Nova Rifle's Type-3 Artillery, the opponent was forced into returning fire. The battle seemed poised to be a long-ranged one—and in that instant, Kuon, having made a wide circle to the left, came swirling into the locked-down enemy position. What impressed him so much was how they never once let the enemy detect his approach.

Fuji had once said, "If the Control is steady and my team is good, the attackers can focus on the enemy in front of them. I'm always looking for ways to make that possible." Remembering that, Kuon took down all four opponents.

In class team combat the next day, Kuon's team scored his first victory with him in Control.

"He can do Control, too... I knew it... Okegawa Kuon's a genius..."

"No, he's a Division 1! Talent's got nothing to do with it."

"That's just even more impressive! I'd legitimately forgotten that till you brought it up."

When En heard his classmates' opinions, she gave a smug little snort.

INTERMISSION: HANABI'S DIARY 3 \\\\\\\\\

Imperial Era 356. May 10th. Suzuka Hanabi.

Kuon-kun's improving so quickly. His Fencing means he's always great in close combat, but now he's learning to make situational decisions. Learning how to Control is undoubtedly making him stronger.

Kuon-kun has started teaching me Fencing. We've barely scratched the surface, but I want to learn whatever I can. He said I've got what it takes. Maybe he just knows when to flatter me. I can't let it go to my head and skip out on practice.

Learning Fencing means I often end up holding Kuon-kun's hands. They're so small, but warm and strong, and covered in calluses. They're the hands of a swordsman.

I love the way his hands tell how he refused to give up because of the magic he was born with and threw himself into the work required to compensate.

Not *that* kind of love!

UNOFFICIAL RECORDS

Imperial Air Force: Assault Reconnaissance Unit. Today's MIA Count: 12.

After a month, Kuon was getting used to life at the Academy.

After school one day, the squad gathered in the meeting room.

"Today, we're going to the sea," Fuji said, with exactly the same gentle smile he always used.

"The sea?" Kuon asked. Naturally, the Jogen Islands were surrounded by water.

Fuji's unwavering smile was almost sparkling. "Time for a little R&R," he answered.

This was definitely a bad idea, Kuon thought.

The suit Rin provided was so ridiculously skimpy. Usually, Fuji could be relied upon to stop this sort of thing, but he was off somewhere with a classmate and showed no signs of returning. Kuon just stood there turning red, so the Warrior Princess Suzuka Hanabi ended up accepting the bikini rather calmly. It was less a bikini and more like a set of strings which apologetically included a few triangles of cloth.

Senpai, are you really going to wear that? Kuon thought. *Are you really going to swim around in that?*

They'd been rocked on a boat for thirty minutes, traveling from the school to the Motegi family's private beach. This was Rin's family property, and Hanabi had lived with her since she was young. They were like sisters and knew their way around. They entered the villa like they owned the place, and, after taking the bikini, Hanabi disappeared behind the curtain they were using in place of a changing room.

Kuon heard the rustle of cloth. Behind the curtain, Hanabi was undressing, about to put on that string bikini.

Senpai, other Lunatic Order Cavalleria are here with us! Lots of boys! Are you really going to wear that?

There were several moments where he almost said something but swallowed his words. Or rather, he began opening his mouth and Rin put him in a chokehold to silence him. Her arm tight around his neck, Rin whispered, "You want to see Hanabi be really cute?"

The whisper of the devil.

"I'm not just talking about a lot of skin here. Hear me out, Kyuu-kun. You know how boys have a beast mode and a sage mode? Well, Hanabi's got two faces to her, too."

Kuon frowned. What could that mean?

Rin winked. "Just you watch. You'll see how cute the Warrior Princess can be."

That wink wasn't reassuring. Rin's grin was downright diabolical.

This is definitely *a bad idea.*

All eight Lunatic Order squads were here. Thirty Cavalleria (genders split evenly) all playing at the beach, with Rin having fed Hanabi a line about it being composure training and puting her in a bikini that left her nearly naked.

Not to be outdone, Rin wore a one-piece suit with a large circle in the front like one of those bubble nudes. It looked far more scandalous than actual nudity, but she wore it with confidence.

A moment later, Fuji came running in with bath towels. "What if somebody saw you?!"

"We haven't even shown anyone yet! We only just put them on!"

Rin's and Fuji's arguments didn't seem to be connected to each other. Fuji tried physically dragging her back inside, but Rin began shrieking about sexual harassment and abuse of power.

Hanabi stepped between them, her exposed body gleaming like the summer sun. "Now, now, both of you calm down," she said.

"Ah!" Fuji's finger caught the string on her back. It stretched taut and gave way. Other Cavalleria heard the noise and turned to stare.

Kuon was certain he'd never moved faster in all his life.

He put all the leg training he'd done into covering the five steps between them in a single bound, grabbing the flying bath towel out of mid-air and covering Hanabi with it. In that, he was successful, but his landing, less so. He landed off-balance and crashed into Hanabi, bath towel and all.

"Mmmph?!"

Hanabi had been standing proudly with her legs apart as the suit peeled away. As Kuon tumbled toward her, he found his vision filled with flesh tones. There was a thump, something that could be described as a boing, and he found himself diving head-first between her gazongas.

There was a blast of hot sand on his face. His nose filled with the smell of the surf and the sweet scent all women have. The sunlight bounced off the glittering surface of the water, and, for a second, he caught a glimpse of the incredibly blue water over yonder.

Then he fell, his face surrounded by sweet-smelling softness.

To anyone watching, it seemed like Kuon had not only torn Hanabi's suit off, but also pushed her over into the sand. The bath towel landed on top of them, hiding both Kuon as well as Hanabi's boobs.

Above him, Hanabi nodded once. "Hmm," she said.

Kuon didn't dare move. If he tried getting up, the bath towel on his head may slip away and expose Hanabi's naked flesh to the world. He moved slightly, looking for a way to slip out from between her breasts without dislodging anything,

"Don't move," Hanabi whispered.

She wrapped the bath towel around herself with Kuon still trapped between her boobs, stood up, and said without the slightest hint of embarrassment, "Excuse me, it seems my suit slipped off. I'll be right back." As Rin, Fuji, and the other Cavalleria stared, stunned, she turned on her heel and walked calmly back inside with Kuon still tucked in the valley of her chest.

Only after Hanabi had calmly left the beach behind, closed the villa door, and locked it behind her did she release the bath towel. The moment Kuon was free, he fell to the floor.

"Um...senpai...?" he asked, hesitantly, unsure why she'd brought him with her.

He'd ended up literally tackling her. There was a good chance she misunderstood his intentions, so he looked up at her with concern...

"..."

...and found the Warrior Princess looking back, her expression totally blank, with two exposed boobs each the size of Kuon's head. He quickly looked down again.

"Kuon-kun?"

"Y-yes...?"

"Did you see my boobs?"

"I did!"

Oops, he thought. He was being too honest again. He stared at the floor, trembling, certain she was going to be furious.

"Ahhhhhhhhhhhhhhhhhhhhhhhhhhhhhhhhhhhhhhhhhhh!!!"

She let out a long, wordless groan, then something moved down into Kuon's field of view. Still half-naked, Hanabi had sat down where she was, and Kuon was now staring at the top of her head.

"Ahhhhhhhhhhhhhhhhhhhh! Hahhhhhhhhhhhhhhhhh!!!"

Her hair swirled around her as she continued listlessly crying out.

"Hanabi-senpai...?"

"Forget it! Forget everything you just saw!"

"Er? Um?"

Kuon wasn't expecting this, and his head was spinning. Although, come to think of it, it was a fairly normal reaction for a girl to have when someone saw her naked. But a second ago, she'd showed no signs of it at all.

"Hanabi-senpai...are...are you embarrassed...?"

She looked up at him, clutching her knees to her chest. From this angle, she looked totally naked. Kuon did his best not to stare at how the flesh of her boobs spilled out as they pressed against her thighs.

"Of course I am!" she said, tears in her eyes. "How could I not be?!"

"B-but a second ago you were totally owning it..."

"Well...everyone was watching, so...I thought I had to act like the school's top Cavalleria... B-but I'm as easily embarrassed as the next girl! I said so before!"

"It does ring a bell..."

A minute ago she'd seemed unflappable, but now, even her ears were red, the very portrait of an embarrassed young maiden. Hard to imagine from the usual Warrior Princess.

This must be what Rin was talking about, Kuon thought. This was Hanabi's other face.

It suddenly struck him as funny. She always seemed like she had it together, but she was just an eighteen-year-old girl. Kuon grinned, forgetting his own age.

"You're adorable, senpai," he said without thinking.

"Wha! W-well, you're a little snot, Kuon-kun!"

"Sorry."

"You aren't sorry at all! I can tell!"

"I am."

"Really?"

"Really."

"Okay then..."

Hanabi's shoulders were shaking. Kuon picked up the bath towel and put it on her. "I'll go get you something to wear." He turned to go find a jacket or something, but Hanabi grabbed his arm. "Senpai?"

She looked up at him, pleading with tears in her eyes. "J-just... stay with me a little longer."

He could hardly refuse. "Of course." He sat down next to her. Hanabi gave him a sideways glance.

"You're very strange, you know."

"How so?"

"I just can't believe you're younger than me. It's like..." She buried her cheek in her knee. "Being with you makes me feel calm."

Was that something he should be happy about? Like, as a man?

Sitting in the villa on the Motegi private beach, a thirty-minute boat ride from Jogen Academy, Kuon stared up at the ceiling, pondering the question as best he could given the naked girl clutching her knees next to him.

It was several minutes before Fuji finished chewing Rin out and the two of them knocked on the door they were leaning on. Neither Kuon nor Hanabi said a word in that time.

It was a good kind of silence.

Some time passed. One day, after school...

"Today, we're going to the sea," Fuji said, with exactly the same gentle smile he always had. The squad had gathered in the meeting room.

"The sea?" Kuon asked. Hadn't they just done that?

His smile never wavering, Fuji pointed downward.

"No," he answered. "The Deep Sea."

A Division Maneuver could function in all environment types: land, water, sky, outer space, and even the deep sea.

This was made possible by a magical barrier called the Witch Bubble. This bubble deflected any and all attacks from the outside, could withstand the water pressure in the ocean depths, and wouldn't let heat or air escape even in regions so deep light couldn't reach them. Their frames provided temperature controls and a breathing environment, and allowed Maneuver Cavalleria to move freely in the deep sea.

That is, as long as their magic held out.

"Got it? Make absolutely sure you don't run out of magic!" Fuji said for the fifth time. "If your bubble vanishes, the water pressure will crush you flat like a sumo wrestler falling on a cake! In an emergency, grab onto someone! If the signal reads as friendly, we can share bubbles. Understood?"

"Yes!"

"Today we'll be doing a patrol of these waters with our senpai from the First Mobile Unit. Treat it like any other patrol, but do *not* let your magic run out! If your DM is released, you die!"

"R-right!"

As Fuji and Kuon belabored the point, the girls shook their heads.

"Leader, he's scared enough."

"At this rate Kyuu-kun's just gonna get all stressed out."

"Mm? Oh...right, Okegawa-kun. Let's have fun! But if your magic runs out, you die."

"I knowwwwww!"

Jogen Island, Imperial Air Force, Wharf #4:

Less than an hour ago, a massive 219-meter-long ship—the Mobile Mothership *Kuou*—had pulled slowly out to sea. The ship was as red as the kanji in its name implied. It served as the mothership for the Division Maneuvers and could fly as well as sail.

The catapults on the stern and prow could launch Cavalleria wearing their DMs, or the *Kuou* could launch small speedcrafts from the lower hatch, as it was doing now. The speedcrafts were stuffed with Cavalleria, and once they reached their destinations and submerged, they'd don their DMs and head for the Deep Sea.

The senpai Fuji had mentioned were four Cavalleria from the Lunar Defense Force, First Mobile Unit, Third Squad. Most Cavalleria in the Lunar Defense Force came from Jogen Maneuver Academy. The Third Squad was no exception. The four of them and the Fuji Squad each boarded a speedcraft and rested until they reached their destination, including Kuon, terrified of operating in the Deep Sea, a place he'd never been in his previous life.

Before the two speedcraft—the *Honoo* and the *Shizuku*—reached the third Danger Zone, the senpai began giving lessons for the frightened Kuon. They were already submerged. In the narrow standby room at the stern of the *Shizuku*, the four members of the Fuji Squad split into two groups, donning their DMs. It was incredibly cramped, so they only had minimal functionality.

Generating only the Core so they could deploy the Witch Bubble and a few small nozzles, they submerged. The standby room slowly filled with seawater. Within their bubbles, the Cavalleria didn't get wet at all, proving the invisible magic barriers were there after all. Then, the airlock opened.

Blackness...

The space yawning open before his eyes was even darker than Kuon had imagined. Darkness beyond the reach of sunlight only fanned the flames of his fear, but he could hardly back out now.

He just had to hope he didn't end up squashed.

He cautiously followed Fuji outside the craft. The buoyancy and water pressure were immense, but the stabilizer functions equipped to his DM made it even easier to control than on land.

"Okay, Okegawa-kun? Do *not* let your magic run out unless you want to die!"

His eighth warning.

Holding onto the bars by the craft's hatch with all his might, Kuon nodded earnestly, on the verge of tears.

Kuon was only a Division 1. He had less magic than all the other Cavalleria; even less magic than your average middle-aged dude. It was less than a thousandth of what Fuji and Rin had, and less than ten thousandths of what Hanabi had. Hanabi could survive out here ten thousand times as long as he could. He was doomed.

But Fuji insisted he'd be fine as long as he didn't unduly exert himself. To Kuon, this sounded like the sort of thing a doctor would say to a terminally ill patient being temporarily discharged from the hospital, but he had nothing else to cling to. He wasn't going to exert himself—at all.

But...

"Bogey on the radar. Three...no, four. Headed right for Jogen."

Intel gathered by the functions on her Division 5 all-rounder frame sent Hanabi into full Cavalleria mode.

This was a patrol.

Their mission was to locate and exterminate stray Jave in the waters around Jogen. They were common enough, whether looking for humans to pick off or for non-human prey. The islands had auto-response systems, but they didn't function this deep, so it was up to the Cavalleria to exterminate the monsters down here.

This was a real fight.

The Division Maneuvers' mobile thrusters and magic light beams were unaffected by the water around them. This day would be both Kuon's first Deep Sea excursion and his first taste of actual combat. He felt like a little kid raising his hand on the first day of school.

"Sensei...does 'combat' count as undue exertion?" he asked, white as a sheet.

"It's not exactly a marathon. Hardly even counts as exercise. Come on, Kuon-kun," Hanabi said. She smiled and took his hand. "This'll be a walk in the park."

Their bubbles merged, and the mobility limit displayed on

Kuon's visor grew by five thousand. Hanabi was sharing her magic with him.

"Feel safer now?" She gave his hand a squeeze, staying resolutely in Bushi Mode.

"Uh, yes..."

It was Kuon who found his heart acting like that of a blushing maiden. If their genders were flipped, this would have been instant love. *My prince...*

Hanabi smiled and joined her other hand to his. She opened the wings on her DMs back and sped up, carrying him with her. The others were already moving ahead, having left Kuon in her care.

When they reached the combat zone, their senpai from the Third Squad had already exterminated the Jave.

The patrol resumed. Each DM was at minimal deployment, following the route at cruising speed. They formed a diamond with their senpai at the head, keeping a close eye on their radar screens. Kuon stayed between Hanabi on the left flank and Fuji in the rear.

They were a thousand meters down. Kuon could see well enough through his DM, considering the minimal light sources. He was in good shape.

Feeling less stressed about it now, he peeled off from Hanabi, moving through the water on his own. Like Fuji had said repeatedly, so long as Kuon was moving steadily, his magic wasn't depleted all that much. If they'd been on the surface, it would have just been a normal expenditure. He considered deploying his Blade and trying out a few moves, but they were on alert, so he'd have to do that later. *Oh, a group of big, ugly fish,* Kuon thought as he peered out into the waters. *Bet they taste terrible.*

He had no idea the senpai flanking him were talking in a private channel.

Hanabi kept an eye on her left flank as she sent a message to Fuji. The Lunar Defense Force proper didn't have a single Division 5, nor did they have a DM with detection functions as advanced as her Reimei.

"What's going on, Fuji-kun? Why are we suddenly doing an ocean patrol?"

There was some fuzz on the channel when Fuji answered. "I don't know. I told them we had a newbie and they should ask someone else, but here we are anyway. The other squads will be doing this starting tomorrow. Either they want to strengthen their guard however they can, or..."

"Or they're looking for students they can use."

"Yeah. That number's been going up lately. Might be time."

"I thought it was still a ways off..."

"The day I chose this path, I knew it would happen someday. You felt the same, right?"

Hanabi was silent.

"Suzuka-kun?"

"Oh, no, I did. I mean, if we don't do something, we've got no future."

"We just have to do what needs to be done."

Hanabi paused for a moment. "Have you had this talk with him?"

"I thought I'd leave it to you."

"Why?"

"He's more important to you than he is to us," Fuji said matter-of-factly.

"That's true enough…"

"Make sure you have no regrets."

"Same to you," Hanabi replied. They exchanged glances, then turned their gazes to Kuon, who was happily swimming between them.

"Okegawa Kuon, was it? The new kid."

Forty minutes after the patrol began, as if sensing their focus was beginning to flag, the Third Squad opened a channel to all units. There were no images, just a low female voice.

"Y-yes," Kuon hastily replied.

"I heard this was your first time at sea. Any problems?"

"No, none!"

"The Force has a high opinion of the Fuji Squad, and you've got a rare Division 5. This should be a good experience for you."

"It is!"

There was a pause. "I thought your voice sounded young… I see. You're only thirteen? Guess you're one of the Lunatic Order's hopes for the future." She was apparently reviewing Kuon's file as they spoke.

"Thank you!"

The way she spoke was clearly designed to reduce the tension between them, but Kuon could only give routine answers.

"Heheh. Fuji was much more arrogant."

"Squad Leader Tsukuba, please don't bring that up," Fuji responded, his voice pained. Tsukuba had selected Fuji as her next victim and happily continued teasing him, pleased by his responses.

"What was it you said the first time we took you out on a mission?" she asked him.

"I don't remember."

"You were thirteen, too. You said, 'I'm going to create the strongest Squad in the Lunar Defense Force.'"

"Sorry, but I'm busy monitoring my surroundings."

"Yo, Okegawa! That's weird, isn't it? Not trying to be the best Cavalleria, but trying to make the best Squad? At only thirteen, this guy knew his path in life was that of a commander, not a warrior. The least cute thing ever. Heheheh."

"Uh...okay..." Kuon felt Fuji *had* made the school's best Squad, but he elected not to say so.

"So, what ambitions do you have? What made you enroll in a Cavalleria training school?"

"I... Well..."

Hanabi looked at Kuon expectantly. Even Fuji stopped looking behind them to stare at him. Rin was enjoying the whole situation, and all four senpai Cavalleria were looking at Kuon. Squad Leader Tsukuba stayed facing forward, waiting for Kuon's reply.

Kuon thought about it, although he already knew the answer.

It was the same it had always been: the job left unfinished in his previous life. He'd made it his life goal at the tender age of two years and four months.

"I want to be a Cavalleria so I can kill the Jave Queen when she returns and destroy all the Jave Gates on Earth. I want to drive them all from this world."

His sensors picked up a dolphin's cry in the distance, echoing below them. He looked down and noticed his group was deep within a marine trench. As the mountains looming on either side of him put pressure on Kuon, he realized his senpai had yet to respond.

Had the transmission cut out? No, there was just a long silence, then...

"*Hah* hahahaha! Hahhh hahahahahahahahahaha!"

Uproarious laughter spilled over the comms. Even the senpai Cavalleria broke their silence, laughing out loud.

"Huh...?" *Did I say something strange?* Kuon wondered, forgetting for a moment he was a mere Division 1.

Floating behind his head, En sighed softly so no one could hear her.

"There's no way you can destroy the Gates! Even the Hero couldn't do that!"

"And as a Division 1? Hahahaha, my sides! That's too funny!"

"It's good to dream big, but maybe try making it a little realistic, ya no-talent Division 1!"

"Heheheh, that's enough, now. He's just a child. He doesn't know everything."

The Third Squad kept laughing like this was the funniest thing they'd ever heard.

Hanabi listened in sullen silence, and when she reached the limits of her patience—as if they were laughing at her own dream—she finally opened her mouth.

"I'm—"

"Hanabi. Don't," Rin said, opening a private comm. Fuji quickly used his rights as a leader to lock down Hanabi's comms. He avoided her eyes. Nothing Hanabi said would reach the Third Squad.

Enraged, Hanabi tapped her controls twice, opening channels to both of them. "Don't you stop me! Let me speak!" she yelled.

"Nope. Not happening," Fuji told her. "I don't want to see you repeat a year, Hanabi. We all need to graduate together."

"Argh!"

If a student squad got into it with a real squad, they'd be penalized. They were only here for training, visiting their future workplace like any other students. They were being allowed to participate in the military's strategy. If the students disobeyed their superiors in any way, the school would come down on them, hard. If they were lucky, they'd only be held back a year. If they weren't so lucky, they'd be expelled.

"You were gonna send your Servants out to smack 'em one, right?" Rin asked. "Even if they didn't fire the second they moved toward that squad, you'd be sunk. Normally you wouldn't just be expelled from the school, you'd be kicked out of the Jogen

Islands." Truthfully, they were unlikely to be that harsh with the best Division 5 the school had ever produced, but Hanabi didn't know that.

"That's...true, but...how did you know..."

Her reluctant admittance was a sign her head had cooled. Rin finally looked at Hanabi and stuck her tongue out. "Because I almost shot a mock bullet at them myself."

Fuji shook his head, sighing. "The two of you...honestly..."

Then Kuon's voice came over the comms as he opened a channel to the three of them. "Um...why is everyone laughing?" he asked, having been excluded from their conversation.

It was clear he genuinely had no idea, so Rin and Fuji both laughed, too. Only Hanabi looked deeply hurt. She turned toward Kuon...

...and that was how she noticed his reaction.

As his comms filled with laughter, Kuon sighed to himself. *I did it again. It's been a while since anyone's laughed this hard at me.*

At school, people had stopped treating him like a child, so he'd let his guard down. In a world where magic power was everything, everyone felt free to laugh at any Division 1.

It was frustrating, but that was all it was. Even Suzuka Hachishiki probably would have done the same thing. Maybe he wouldn't have even noticed someone like Kuon.

His school—no, his *squad*—were too kind. They all treated a Division 1 like himself too warmly. Most people would react like these senpai had.

It made sense; he told himself it made sense. He'd convinced himself it had, in theory.

Kuon's memories and soul were Suzuka Hachishiki's, but his magic and body were his own, so his body reacted its own way. His vision grew blurry. *Weird,* he thought, then felt his cheeks grow damp. He suddenly realized Hanabi was right next to him. "Senp—"

"You know what I think, Kuon-kun?"

During a mission, it was forbidden to disrupt the formation, especially for personal reasons, but Hanabi didn't give a damn about any of that now.

Okegawa Kuon had been laughed at, hurt, and was crying alone in the dark of the ocean while trying not to let the others know. Once she saw that, Hanabi was ready to toss everything else out the window.

Their bubbles merged. Hanabi reached out both hands and cupped Kuon's face between them. She smiled, speaking to him and him alone.

"I believe you can do it. Maybe it'll take time. Maybe you'll fail a lot along the way. But I think you *will* pull it off. I've watched you long enough to know that much."

She understood. She believed.

She wiped his tears away with her fingers and went back to her position. Whether they'd seen him crying or not, none of the senpai scolded Hanabi for breaking formation.

Kuon's memories and soul might be Suzuka Hachishiki's, but his magic and body weren't.

His tears kept falling, some of them out of happiness.

The patrol went smoothly after that. They had two further encounters, but neither significant; the Fuji Squad remained on standby the entire time.

Kuon's tears had long since dried.

INTERMISSION: HANABI'S DIARY 4 \\\\\\\

Imperial Era 356. May 13th. Suzuka Hanabi.

Kuon-kun cried. I've never seen him cry before. The way I felt wasn't...sad so much as...anguished?

I said what I needed to say but arghhhhhhhhhhhh I put both hands on his faaaaaaaaaaaaaaaaaaace and his tears were just aughhhhhhhhhhh why did I do that while our senpai were waaaaaaaaaatching?!

I began clutching my head in bed and my roommate Rin gave me a weird look. She threw her arms around me, so I said, "I don't wanna wrestle, go away," which she did, but still looked very crafty.

Oh dear.

I'd better change my diary password just in case.

999999999

I just typed "9" nine times. I dunno why, lately I just really like the number nine.

Not because it's in Kuon's name!

INTERMISSION: ????

She was scrolling through someone else's diary.

Not wanting to wake her roommate up, she kept the room in darkness, aside from the device window.

"She's only writing about Kyuu-kun."

The diary-reading, glasses-wearing girl laughed to herself. She got to the denial at the end and wrote "www" after it, netslang for laughter.

Then she wrote, "Liar! www" under that but figured that would get her caught and deleted it.

"Enjoy being young, Hanabi."

Maybe her roommate was dreaming about something. She sure was smiling a lot in her sleep.

UNOFFICIAL RECORDS

Imperial Air Force: Assault Reconnaissance Unit. Today's MIA Count: 15.

Meat Pillar believed to be a control device discovered near the Gate.

INTERMISSION: HANABI'S DIARY 4: POSTSCRIPT

How sleepy was I to type "www" after that last entry? World Wide Web?

It was June, and Suzuka Hanabi and Headmaster Nanahoshi Kaede were set for an exhibition match.

The news took the school by storm. The origins of it were unclear, but it was spread by the high school's goofball newspaper club with the following copy:

The strongest Cavalleria in school history versus the strongest human alive! Which of them will emerge victorious? A blood-soaked cat-fight for the ages! Time to SETMA!

(SETMA was short for "SETtle this in a Division MAneuver.")

Like so much other news, this information was somewhat incorrect. In fact, it would be a mock battle of the four members of the Fuji Squad versus the headmaster, solo. The Fuji Squad had been ranked at the top of the Lunatic Order for so long, Kaede was just itching to kick their asses and get some drive back into them. The truth caused another stir around the school, and although the odds initially favored Nanahoshi Kaede, they began to even out a bit. The newspaper club served as the bookie, and all proceeds would wind up greasing their club funds.

The result was a landslide. The fight lasted a mere one minute and seventeen seconds.

The students were relieved, reassured that not only had they joined the right school, but the government made the right choice when they installed Nanahoshi Kaede as headmaster.

She was still the world's greatest Cavalleria.

The world's greatest Cavalleria was also the world's greatest lecturer, as the Fuji Squad were finding out. They were gathered in the ridiculously high-ceilinged headmaster's office, sitting on their knees as Kaede chewed them out.

"Kuon, you still can't stop yourself from charging in like an idiot, you idiot.

"Hanabi, I know your Fencing is still rudimentary, but try not to telegraph everything, you idiot.

"Rin, you rely too much on your skill with a sniper. Attack more and put the pressure on, you idiot.

"But the ultimate idiot is the idiot carrying all you idiots... Fuji, you idiot. Your schemes are obvious as hell and, as soon as one goes wrong, you leave it up to everyone's individual abilities. How stupid can you be? You knew I'd use Seven-Count Strike, so trying to shoot back head-on was really hopeless. I said at the start, 'Pretend you ain't fighting a human and come at me like you would the Jave.' Only a total idiot would try and fight them fairly, you nitwit."

Fuji was repeatedly smacked on the head with a rolled-up magazine. As the Squad Leader, full responsibility fell unto him. He was clearly ready to burden it, looking remorseful and repeatedly nodding and saying, "Yes, as you say," and, "Sorry," at random.

Kuon knew better than to say anything, but he couldn't stop himself. "Um, Master, Seven-Count Strike is definitely going a bit too far."

"Two hundred Sword Swings," Kaede said, not even looking back from the cadence she was tapping on the handsome leader's head.

"Huh?"

"Penalty for talking back. Get a sword. Swing it 300 times."

"The number went up?"

"Sword. Swing. Four hun—"

"Uh, yes, Headmaster! Starting three hundred swings right nowww!"

Kuon rose straight from kneeling to standing, grabbed the lightest looking sword from the inexplicable array of swords decorating the wall, and began swinging.

"Not that one, idiot," Kaede said, and pointed at a ridiculously heavy-looking, two-meter-long sword. "That one."

Tired before he even began, Kuon began swinging. "One..."

"I can't hear you! Add fifty more!"

"ONE! TWO! THREE! FOUR!" Kuon shouted, despairing. Why did he have to swing a three-kilogram sword right in front of his senpai during the already sad post-match meeting?

The way Rin was trying to hide a smirk infuriated him. Kuon's "THIRTEEN!" and the *bonk* of the magazine on Fuji's head were in such perfect sync that if they were playing Pop'n Music, the "PERFECT" text would have appeared on screen. Stealing a look at Hanabi's immobile Bushi serenity, Kuon swung a thirty-fourth time.

Nanahoshi Kaede was Division 4.

Normally, there was no way a Division 5 like Hanabi would ever lose to Kaede's magic, even one-on-one. Unlike her match with Kuon, she'd gone for every advantage she had and attacked at a distance. She'd still lost.

Each Division level's magic potential increased exponentially as it went up. Defining it in terms of speed, Division 1 was a slug, Division 2 a crawling baby, Division 3 a human running at 1kph, Division 4 a car driving at 100 kph, and Division 5 an airplane going 1000 kph. Each Division level higher was a taller and thicker wall to overcome.

Therefore, it was harder to beat someone whose Division was higher than you, and that became worse the higher the Division. This was common sense; it was in their textbooks.

But Nanahoshi Kaede was a genius who defied common sense; the strongest human alive.

Seven-Count Strike was a special weapon specially designed for Shichisei Kenbu users. Kaede had it equipped to her custom-made DM, Kyokai (Pleiades), and it could very well have been the secret to her strength.

This weapon had the power to raise her Division Level to 5 for seven seconds.

Kaede had used this and her Shichisei Kenbu arts to utterly trounce Suzuka Hanabi. Only a master of Shichisei Kenbu could use this unique weapon. It required such a huge volume of magic that even a Division 5 didn't have enough.

So, how was a Division 4 using it? Kaede had already told Kuon the reason. When she gave him his Guide, En, she'd said, "One of the Shichisei Kenbu ultimate arts is a breathing technique which reduces magic expenditure by 1 *kei*. I know a certain idiot who got himself kicked out before he learned it."

That idiot was currently using his reincarnated body to swing a sword, but Nanahoshi Kaede knew that only an idiot who'd bet his entire life on obsessive training could ever learn the Shichisei Kenbu ultimate arts. She'd even done it herself.

Kaede stopped playing *Taiko no Tatsujin* with Fuji's head and looked at her beloved student, muttering, "Eight follows seven. And nine follows eight."

The "nana" in "Nanahoshi" was the kanji for seven. The "ha-chi" in "Hachishiki" was the kanji for eight. If one were to replace the "ku" in "Kuon" with the kanji for nine...

The day would soon come when Kuon would inherit the name, the sword, and the special weapon.

Her idiot student swung his sword. "One hundred nine!" he shouted.

"Too quiet! Again!"

"NIIIIIINE!"

"Again!"

"NIIIIIIIIIIIIIIIIIIIIIIIIIIIIIIIIIIIIIIIIIIIIIIIIIIIINE!"

"Kuon."

"NIIIIIIIIIIIIIIIIIIIIIIIIIIIIIIIIIIIIIIIIIIIIIIIIIIIIIINE!"

"Good luck."

"One hun—wait, whaaat? There's no way my master would ever say *that*!"

"Add another fifty."

"ONE HUNDRED ELEVEEEEEEEEEEEEEEEEEEEEEEEE EEEEEN!"

Shortly afterward, Kaede told Kuon he was in the way of her work, so he should do the rest at home. She sent the rest of the Fuji Squad packing.

Weird. It's like she's becoming...nicer? Kuon wasn't sure if that was a good thing or a warning that something incredibly terrifying was coming, which just showed how thorough her education had been.

As it turned out, the latter hunch was correct.

JUNE GAVE WAY TO JULY, and the gap between deep sea patrols was growing shorter.

The First Mobile Unit had begun forming and reforming squads. Official records showed their total numbers were unchanged, but the number of squads was diminishing—there had been ten, but now were only six. Yet the squads the Fuji Squad accompanied only ever had four in them. If the official total number of Cavalleria hadn't changed, the number of people in each squad should have increased...if those official numbers were accurate.

Our senpai look exhausted, thought Kuon. They clearly hadn't been getting any rest at all, and others were beginning to notice. Perhaps the Lunar Defense Force was engaged in some major strategy and pulling staff from patrols to shore that up.

Then there were ten squads again, but the number in each was halved. In other words, to increase the total number of patrols, they were running at half the personnel. It looked as though they were adjusting for the loss of power by using the student squad members who'd simply waited on standby before now.

The two members of the Third Squad were flying ahead of the Fuji Squad: the female Squad Leader, Tsukuba, and one other senpai Cavalleria.

This was their fourth patrol this month. They were both far too stressed to joke around. Even if they found a stray Jave, unless it was really close to Jogen, they avoided engagment.

But that backfired on them.

The Jave surrounded them before Hanabi had even noticed. Patrols following set routes were easily subverted, even by monsters with as little intelligence as the Jave. If they'd defeated the enemies as Hanabi detected them one by one, they'd never have had to face this many at once.

Too late now.

There were sixty Jave in total, outnumbering the Cavalleria ten to one. All hope faded from Tsukuba's face, but she quickly replaced it with grim determination. Her own life may end in disgrace, but she *would* find a way to let the students escape.

"We'll buy you time to get away," she ordered, the sort of line one only heard in movies.

"Even B-movies have better dialogue these days, Squad Leader Tsukuba," Fuji said.

"Shut up and go!"

The enemy were closing in. The Jave weren't yet visible to the naked eye, but their DMs were projecting expanded area information onto their fields of vision, and the monsters encircling them were stretching tentacles their way. There were more monsters above. There was no time to waste arguing, or even to say any last words.

The Lunatic Order leader persevered. "In real B-movies, they say this: 'Permission to speak freely? Requesting command.'"

"What?"

"You're planning on dying here?" Fuji asked.

"So?"

"Let's assume you're already dead and let me have command."

"Don't you get it? I'm telling you to run while you still can!"

"And I'm saying we can win."

"How—"

"Okegawa-kun!" Fuji yelled, interrupting Tsukuba. No point in arguing about it further. "We're doing this. You ready?"

They were out of time. Fuji began barking his orders. "Okegawa-kun at the center with Suzuka-kun locked onto him. Motegi-kun and I will be front and rear. Squad Leader Tsukuba—"

"What are you thinking?!" Tsukuba shouted.

"It's too late to run either way. I'd like you on the right and left. We're ready to start."

Their alerts sounded; the Jave were in range. Tsukuba grit her teeth and gave the order. "Suit yourself!"

"Thank you. Your combat abilities are invaluable, and I intend on bringing you back alive."

Elbow out to the side, he put his closed fist to his chest in a Cavalleria salute. Then, Fuji flew forward.

Okegawa Kuon's Shichisei Kenbu was about to begin.

Kuon and Hanabi merged bubbles once more, holding hands. This established a magical link between them.

Next, Hanabi deployed Reimei's Servants, attaching them to the four Cavalleria around them. Now all the squad members had a magical link to Kuon through Hanabi.

This was the start of Kuon's Shichisei Kenbu Link Art.

Shichisei Kenbu: Mod. Tensetsu Shigure.

When he first fought Hanabi, the two of them had resonated, and Hanabi's vision had linked to Kuon's time stop. When Fuji heard about this from Kuon, he jumped on it. He theorized that, by using the bubble to link their magic, Kuon would be able to share Tensetsu with everyone's senses.

It worked.

Six Cavalleria's visions went white.

The blackness of the deep sea reversed, turning a bright white. The thick lines running everywhere were predicted enemy attacks. Several of them pierced the six DMs, and the flat, belt-like lines were Kuon's calculated evasion routes. Simply sharing his vision wasn't enough to give everyone an evasion line. Even so, what felt like forty-three seconds of frozen time combined with a 98 percent accurate future prediction was enough to dramatically increase the survival and victory rates for the entire Squad.

The two senpai wasted the first thirty seconds on confusion. Fuji hadn't had the time to explain at all. Still, they instinctively realized those thick lines should be dodged, and spent the remaining thirteen seconds calculating how to do so.

Rin's task was simple: avoid the piercing lines, twist her frame into a space with no lines running through it, then fire at the Jave approaching from the front, shooting from right to left.

Fuji took full advantage of the forty-three seconds. Like Kuon, he calculated his own evasion routes, but he had planned them out far further than Kuon did. He calculated fourteen patterns by which all six allies could safely move before time ran out.

Hanabi didn't share this vision. Her time never stopped. She was right in front of Kuon, with her hands held in his. She was staring right at him, but since she didn't share the time stop, her eyes couldn't follow him.

Kuon's job was already done. The first step of Fuji's proposal for using Tensetsu Shigure to attack in all directions involved Kuon doing nothing but stopping time and sharing the attack lines with all the squad members. He instead spent the entire forty-three seconds staring at Hanabi. It was almost voyeuristic, and he felt a little guilty about it. He knew he was being a real creep, but what else could he look at when someone this beautiful was in front of him? He'd have to apologize to her later. How would she respond?

Tensetsu released, and time resumed.

Instantly, the four Cavalleria around him moved without hesitation. The two senpai Cavalleria easily evaded the Jave's light beams. Rin not only evaded them, she dove into the hail of it all, all of which missed. She took up a sniping position and fired into the paths the Jave were heading toward. Fuji saw how his team had responded and decided the third pattern was most appropriate. He stayed still so as to not get in the way and waited for the right moment.

Hanabi's Servants moved away from the other four. Kuon

breathed out. Hanabi's eyes were following his again. She nodded. He breathed in.

Shichisei Kenbu: Mod. Tensetsu Shigure.

A second Tensetsu. This time stop was just for Kuon and
Hanabi. They could both see the Jave's attack lines, and the future
lines for their allies who'd already committed to attacks.

This meant no misfires.

Kuon calculated shot routes and shared them with Hanabi.
These traced the same arcs as the Shichisei Kenbu major art Shijin
Reppakuzan, which Suzuka Hachishiki had once used. These
lines depicted a massive attack range, and Hanabi saw them and
understood.

Forty-three seconds later, the flow of time in the deep sea returned to normal. Hanabi let go of Kuon's hands, put her Scout
Nova Rifle in her right hand, and held out her left, palm open,
focusing the aim of her Servants. Without a moment's hesitation,
she fired.

Two beams of light raced across the blackness as if bound
for the distant horizon. The first was the massive beam fired out
of Hanabi's rifle, unaffected by the water. The second, a concentrated beam created by merging the Servants' microbeams into
one, like the focused setting on an adjustable showerhead. The
twin beams swallowed up all the Jave at the four and ten o'clock
directions, exterminating them.

Then her light turned. Precisely following the shot routes
Kuon had showed her, Hanabi swept her beams left, right, up,
and down. The Jave in the water, and the Jave floating above

hoping to chomp on the Cavalleria as they ascended—none of them could react in time to avoid the sudden burst of deadly light.

By the time the lights stopped racing everywhere, the sixty Jave in the water around them had been annihilated, reduced to a fine crimson mist.

It took some time before Tsukuba understood what had just happened. Time had suddenly stopped, she'd dodged the first attack, then light flickered everywhere and, before she knew it, there were no enemies left. She had no idea what they'd done.

As she drifted in a dazed silence, Fuji saluted.

"Squad Leader Tsukuba, I'm glad to see you safe."

There is a current known as the "Magnetic Stream." It was discovered shortly after mankind first took a Division Maneuver to the deep sea. Also known as the Deep Sea Mud Stream, it is generated by the waxing and waning of the moon, by deep sea currents, and by DM combat actions. It races around the seas near Jogen like a storm, absorbing magic everywhere it goes.

The Cavalleria had not taken it into consideration during their battle.

The Jave were gone, and nothing was on Hanabi's radar. They'd just decided to call off the patrol, return to the speedcraft, and head back to the *Kuou* when the Magnetic Stream blew through the ocean.

Kuon was caught by the wave, as was Hanabi when she tried saving him, and the two of them were swept away from the group by a current traveling faster than the speed of sound. It was over in an instant.

The Witch Bubble was made of and powered by magic. A Cavalleria could never let their magic run dry in the deep sea, as they had to keep their protective bubbles up.

The Magnetic Stream, however, washes away magic.

The Witch Bubble popped.

Senpai!

Kuon-kun! Kuon-kun, Kuon-kun!

Somehow, despite the violent current, they managed to catch each other's hands. They then let the storm carry them. Kuon only had a little magic left, so if Hanabi hadn't been swept away with him, he would have been dead in a matter of minutes. Hanabi had saved him from the brink of death, but, emotionally speaking, she felt the exact opposite. Their bubbles merged and she threw her arms around Kuon, shaking like a leaf. She buried her face in his chest and cried her eyes out. Kuon's mind was a total blank, so all he could do was cradle her head and listen to her.

The bubble drifted deep into the ocean. Kuon watched helplessly as they were yanked into terrifying darkness, down to the depths of the Mariana Trench. He reached up toward the surface, but it was beyond him. The sun, the light... All of it grew further and further away.

Fortunately, a DM's Witch Bubbles were ridiculously hardy. When they reached a depth of 10,000 meters, Kuon sat surrounded by darkness, reminded that these strange bubbles could even sustain life in the void of space.

"Senpai, are you okay?" he asked.

Hanabi was lying in his arms, like he was a knight carrying his princess. Inside the Maneuver, she weighed nothing. She nodded and quietly apologized, never letting go of his hand. She took a few deep breaths and looked up.

"Sorry, Kuon-kun. I panicked."

She seemed like her old self—but wasn't. She was just faking it, doing her best to keep it together. Kuon could still feel her shoulders shaking.

"We've been swept a long way," she said. "This must be the bottom of a trench... Let's rest a bit, recover some magic, then head up and get back to the ship. We'll see if we can contact anyone."

The way she still tried acting like a senpai was both reliable and loveable.

"Are you hurt at all, Kuon-kun?" she asked him.

"No, thanks to you. But my frame..." *Was destroyed,* he finished silently. Pretty much the only thing Kuon's Soukyu (Mod) could do was put out a minimal bubble. It was a starter's Division 1 frame and was super fragile.

"Okay. We'll be fine as long as we stay linked."

Hanabi nodded firmly in his arms. Her own arms were still clutching around him like a little girl. Only her words were those of a confident Bushi.

"Rations will help recover magic. Do you have any? If not, you can have half of mine."

The Witch Bubble floated through the water. They left it to its natural buoyancy, letting it slowly rise as they pressed tightly against each other.

Like a knight and a princess.

Even in these dire straits, Hanabi smelled nice. Kuon knew she was in great shape, yet it always surprised him how soft she felt. Worst of all was that, from this angle, every time he looked down, he saw the valley of her breasts laid out before him.

Hanabi looked up, catching his eye. "Kuon-kun?"

"Yes! Sorry!"

"For what...?"

"Nothing!"

She looked confused, but soon forgot it. "I can't get at the rations from this position. Sorry, but can you get them from my hip?"

"Um, sure?"

Rustle rustle.

"Eeep!" The Warrior Princess suddenly made a noise like a startled cat. "Oh, don't, that tickles!"

"Augh, sorry! I didn't mean to!"

"Ah, ah, ha hya hyaaa! Wh-where are you touching...heee hahaha!"

"S-s-s-s-sorryyy!"

The rations came in a gelatin form, in silver packs you put in your mouth and sucked the contents out of.

Only when he'd finally managed to get the pack out and hand it to her did he realize...

"Um, senpai, we don't actually need to stay like this."

"Should I move away?"

"No, if you did, my bubble would burst, so..." He'd just meant the princess position she was in wasn't necessary. But...

"Can...we stay like this?" she asked.

Mode Change!

This oddly forlorn-looking maiden version of Hanabi looked up at him like a fragile, weakened, lost puppy, and it was so cute Kuon's heart nearly burst. He immediately nodded. "Of course we can."

When they were alone together, she got all clingy...or was that just his imagination?

"Thank you..." she whispered. She put the gelatin pouch to her lips and took a sip.

Kuon went to drink his own, but his hands were full. His right hand was on Hanabi's back and shoulders, and his left under her knees. He wasn't really supporting her—if he took his hands away, she'd stay right where she was—but the moment he tried moving his hand...

"Here, Kuon-kun."

Hanabi held up her pack, the same one that had just been at her lips.

Offering him half.

That's right, she'd said as much. Kuon was silent, his eyes locked on to the silver pouch. Should he? Could he? Adrift 10,000 meters deep with a super-hot senpai offering an indirect kiss? He was thrilled, totally delighted, but...

"Uh, s-sorry..." Hanabi said, taking his silence for refusal. "I guess that was rude."

She looked so dejected that Kuon's heart broke. "No, I'll take it!" he blurted out.

"Huh? Y-you will...? You want a sip...?"

"Yes, I'm all about your kisses!"

"I...don't think that's what we're doing here, but...o-okay..." Hanabi held the nozzle out to him. "H-here..."

Her face turned slightly red, and she wouldn't meet his gaze. Adorable.

"Senpai...you're so beautiful..."

Her fingers.

"D-don't say weird things... Um, Kuon-kun?"

"Yes?"

"D-don't bite..."

"I will suck so gently."

"Um, if it stops coming out then...you can use your tongue to coax the rest out so...lick it...?"

"Got it."

Kuon nodded, and carefully moved his lips to Hanabi's pouch. Her entire body was trembling. He tightened his grip on her shoulders to reassure her.

"Ah..."

He placed his lips on it.

Just as she'd instructed, he ran his tongue along the nozzle, but nothing came out. This thing was playing hard to get. Kuon sucked a little harder. He must have moved his fingers a little on her back, because Hanabi made a noise like he was tickling her.

"Mmmahhh...mm...Kuon-kuuun!"

"Just a little longer, Hanabi-senpai..."

"I said...be gentle, but..."

"I can't stop myself."

"Don't move...your fingers..."

No matter how regal the Warrior Princess might normally be, she was just a cute girl right now. Kuon kept sucking on her offering, not letting it get away.

"Hahhh...Kuon...kuuunnn!"

Hanabi let out a loud wail, and at last a mouthful of gelatin reached Kuon's mouth.

He slurped it up. It was good. Lemon flavored; a little tart.

Kuon took his mouth away from the pouch and spoke to Hanabi, who was trying not to laugh.

"Senpai, this is pretty good!"

"Hah...hah...you won't stop tickling me..."

"I'm sorry."

Kuon now knew Hanabi's back was her weak point. He had no idea if that information would ever be of use.

Then...

"Erm...ahem! Ahem!" En appeared, making a show of clearing her throat.

"H-how long have you been here, En-kun?" Kuon stuttered.

"Since always? The whooole time?"

"You shouldn't surprise people like that! Honestly!"

"That's what I want to say...where do you think we are?"

Hanabi looked around her. "The deep sea...?"

"I don't know how you two can flirt like this 10,000 meters down."

"Flirt? What are you talking about? I was just drinking emergency rations."

"It sure didn't sound like it... But moving right along." En shook her head, muttering softly about how oblivious the two of them were.

"If you're here, En, then are the comms connected?" Hanabi asked.

"Yes, barely," En said, displaying a small headset and mic in one hand. There was a small box in front of her, and she was carefully adjusting its dials like it was a radio or sonar. "Connected. My master is already taking action. I've sent our coordinates, so a rescue should be on its way."

"That's gre—"

"Hanabi! Are you safe?!" Rin's voice was very loud. "Any injuries?! Just sit tight, we'll be right there!"

Video was impossible, but it seemed like audio signals were viable. "Oh, my friend. We're safe, thanks. Kuon-kun is, too."

Rin breathed a sigh of relief. "You're with Kyuu-kun, then?"

"Yes, we managed to stay together."

"Just the two of you?"

"En-kun's here, too!"

"It's going to take us at least three hours to get there. I'm sure you're aware of this, but don't attempt to move unless absolutely necessary."

"We'll try."

"Kyuu-kun, take care of Hanabi."

"I will, Rin-san."

"You can hug her if you have to."

"Er..."

"I wouldn't object to sucking faces, either."

"Huh?"

"H-hanging up now!"

Hanabi cut the transmission before Rin could scream anything more inappropriate, then sighed.

"You've already got your arms around me...but, uh, not like that!"

"D-definitely not!"

"And the only sucking we did was on that ration pouch..."

"Hm? No, senpai, by 'sucking faces' I think she meant...something else."

"Huh? What does that mean, anyw—oh."

"..."

"..."

The two of them turned bright red as En watched with evident enjoyment. "You two are so cute when you get all self-conscious!"

Neither Kuon nor Hanabi could look at each other.

"Um," En said excitedly. "I'll just put myself in sleep mode!"

"Huh? Why?"

"The magic link with my master is tenuous, so maintaining this form is sooo exhausting!"

"You...don't *look* tired..."

"You two go ahead and be young together! Hehehehehehe!"
With a very loaded chuckle, the AI Device vanished.

"…"

"…"

Silences felt especially silent this far underwater.

"S-Senpai, that reminds me…"

"Reminds you of what?!"

"Um…well…uh, right! I've always thought it was weird, but why are there so many enemies around Jogen?"

"O-oh, is that all? That's easy! It's because the front lines are falling back!"

"What…?"

"Ah!" Hanabi's face made it clear that wasn't something she should have shared with him. Kuon dug in, driven by memories from his time as Suzuka Hachishiki and of all the family and fellow orphans and Cavalleria who'd died in his past life.

"What does that mean? 'The front lines are falling back'? There's a front line fighting the Jave? I was told that, thanks to the Hero, the Jave had almost entirely ceased their activities and were sleeping over the capital. Everyone in Jogen knows that. So why?"

"Um, well, you see…" Hanabi began, drooping visibly.

Kuon had no way of knowing how much Hanabi resented being dragged away from more thrilling subjects into this far more important conversation. She didn't want to talk about this at all, but she felt like she had to.

"The Hero did manage to close the Gate temporarily. Thanks to that, the Jave invasion was temporarily suspended. That much is true. However, the seal only lasted ten years. Three years ago, the Gate reopened, and humanity launched into a full-scale war against the Jave."

"But... But nobody knows?"

"Information suppression. We can't tell anyone. With few exceptions, Earth is now a Jave colony. Jogen isn't safe, either. That's why the patrols are increasing."

"Oh, God..."

"You realize, Kuon-kun," Hanabi said, "we call ourselves the Imperial Air Force, but we only have squads in Jogen. We never hear anything about any forces on the mainland."

No.

"Yes," Hanabi nodded wearily. "The Jave control almost all of the Empire. If they're appearing above the water, their main nest must be on the mainland capital. The Lunar Defense Force is working on a large-scale strategy to take it out. The Gate is in the capital, so they want to close it like the Hero once did."

Just as Kuon once had.

I can't do it myself, Kuon thought. Even in the battle in his previous life, it was unclear to him what factor had managed to seal the Gate. He'd destroyed the four flesh pillars around the Gate, hoping they were control panels of some kind, but nothing had happened. Even if they could reach the Gate, it would be no simple matter. Not without a incredibly large force or a Division 5 like Suzuka Hachishiki...

A Division 5?

"Senpai, are you...?"

"Yes. The Fuji Squad's being called up. Don't know when yet."

"We are...?" Then he would be, too. Kuon was ashamed of his recent thoughts. He couldn't do it himself? Wasn't his whole goal to kill the Queen? Plus, sealing the Gate was just as important. If they destroyed the Gate before the Queen returned, that would be even better.

He made up his mind, power welling up within him. He had no intention of wasting his second life.

"I'll lay my life on the line, too. The four of us *will* close that Gate."

Hanabi looked at him apprehensively, as if his very face would blind her. Then she turned her eyes away and hung her head. "You're strong, Kuon-kun," she whispered with a self-deprecating smile. "Joining the Lunatic Order, that Tensetsu just now... Hard to believe you're only thirteen."

"No, I'm—"

"Fuji-kun said almost the same thing you did. Rin, too. Everyone's made up their mind. I'm the only one in the Fuji Squad who's still scared."

"You are...?"

"Sorry, Kuon-kun. You must be disappointed. I always act tough, but I'm actually constantly terrified, even though I'm Division 5. Pathetic, right? The head of the Lunar Defense Force himself told me he wanted me to close the Gate the way the Hero did. But I just... I just can't..."

Hanabi's shoulders were shaking. A single tear rolled down her cheek.

"I just can't find the confidence..."

Kuon knew he had to say something to comfort her, to encourage her, but his mind was drawing a blank. How? What could he say? He didn't know. He had no idea at all.

Kuon couldn't find the words...so he let Suzuka Hachishiki's memories talk instead.

Remember what you used to say at times like this in your last life.

He took a breath.

"We're adrift in the vastness of the ocean. Waiting for rescue in the dark with no idea when enemies will come, only an inexperienced kouhai with you. All of that's enough to make anyone feel uneasy. I won't tell anyone what happened here."

He could tell Hanabi was listening.

"I think you're doing great," he went on. The words were spilling out on their own now. "Being called the strongest in school history, being a rare Division 5—that's a lot of pressure. Pretending to be strong even though you're really scared, working hard not to let your powerful magic go to your head... You're always trying so hard."

He looked up and smiled at her as he wiped away her tears.

"I believe you can do it. And I believe that because I've been watching you all this time."

"That's..." Hanabi said, tears streaming. "That's my..."

The boy was back to being Kuon. He cupped Hanabi's face in his hands. "You'll be fine. I guarantee it."

The waterworks were really flowing now. Hanabi tried wiping away her tears, but she couldn't keep up. Rin had given him permission, so Kuon gave her a tender embrace.

In his arms, his sweet, adorable senpai was nodding to herself. She really did try hard.

He was glad they were so deep in the ocean. Here, even someone as short as him could hold Hanabi's head to his chest.

As they floated slowly toward the surface, he noticed something nigh-miraculous overhead. He pointed up at the circular outline.

"Senpai, look."

They'd come a long way up. The distant sphere of the sun was glowing above. Jellyfish and regular fish swam between them and that glowing orb, like the fish were tracing a circle around it.

It looked like a solar eclipse, a momentary illusion created by the sea. The light reflected by the salt water and the transparent jellyfish enlarged the shadows, creating a large black circle like an eclipse. Okegawa Kuon just thought it was beautiful.

Hanabi though...

A big black moon...

When she saw it, Hanabi's mind suddenly flashed back to when she was five years old.

_//////////

Everywhere was slaughter. Flesh and blood and bone and the remains of humans. The capital, Ginza, turned into a war zone, fires burning. Little Hanabi was surrounded by flames and what was left of her parents.

The smell of iron and burning flesh; the taste of blood and sand; the sound of screams and sirens and massive things dragging.

Everywhere she looked, there were hideous things burning, pitch-black smoke, and swaths of red.

Monstrous red.

Coming closer...

Through the smoke, Hanabi saw something big squeezing through the piles of rubble, dragging itself across the ground on dozens of tentacles, each clutching human heads and limbs. It tossed them into its many mouths, chewing them, swallowing them.

"No..." Hanabi gasped, realizing she would share their fate. "No, no, I don't wanna, I don't wanna! No, no, no, stop!"

She was too scared to take her eyes off it. She just screamed, tears running down her face. She screamed and screamed...

Something slithered across the back of her neck.

She turned around and there they were right in front of her, a whole pack of them. Monster after monster after monster surrounding her. Red, fleshy, people-eating monsters. A terrifying number of tentacles grabbed Hanabi's neck, her arms, and her legs.

She screamed.

She screamed so loud nothing else existed.

Then...

Shichisei Kenbu.

She heard a voice; she thought she was imagining it. There was no one else left alive in this burning city, no one who could save her.

But then a wind blew.

A round disc of wind swirled around her. Like the kamai-tachi of legend, this wind had blades. An instant later, every single one of the gross tentacles was cut down. No, not just the tentacles—all the monsters around her were gone. All that was left was a reddish mist mingling with the smoke. But Hanabi was too young to realize that was proof the monsters had been exterminated.

"Are you okay?"

It was a human, a grown man. He was wearing a large suit of armor, carrying a huge sword, and Hanabi just knew he was the one who had saved her.

She'd seen him before.

"Are you the only survivor?" He went down on one knee to little Hanabi's eye level. She'd seen him on TV. He was a distant relative, the last hope of humanity... A very strong and bad-ass Cavalleria.

Hanabi nodded. He smiled sadly and stood up. He looked around at all the bodies then spoke, as if apologizing. "I'll be with you all soon."

Even at five, she knew what that meant. She knew where he was going. He would be joining her parents and friends and everybody else who had gone...leaving her behind.

She envied his words, the look in his eyes. She thought it would be so much better if she could give up like that.

"Um..."

"Hm?"

Little Hanabi couldn't find the words to express what she was feeling. "Hero, are you gonna die?" she asked.

An oversized moon shone down upon them. They were surrounded by fires and rubble and oh so many bodies.

The Hero put his hand on her head, smiling awkwardly. "You're going to live," he said.

"Just me...?"

"Yes. We at least have to..."

"But... But everyone else is dead..."

Blood and guts were littered all around them. Some were the remains of people gobbled up by the tentacle monsters, and some were bits of the tentacle monsters after the Hero had arrived and torn them apart.

"That's why you need to live," the Hero said. "For all those who didn't."

"You're not coming with me?"

"Sorry. I can't."

"Why not?"

The Hero looked up at the giant moon hanging overhead in broad daylight. The moon was pitch black, glowing around the edges. It was a door leading to the world on the other side, a demonic moon which spit out an endless stream of the tentacle monsters that came to eat them.

A Gate...

To their nest.

"I've got to go avenge everyone."

"Take me with you!" Hanabi cried.

"I can't do that."

"They... They're all dead! Please! I want to die with them! I want to go where they are!"

"I'm sorry..." he apologized, like it hurt to say. The Hero put something in her hands and said, "Division Maneuver, activate."

Instantly, little Hanabi was surrounded by a cocoon of pale light. She began floating. *He's going to send me away, all alone,* she realized. "Hero!"

"This is my gift to you. Get out of this place."

"Wait, please! Don't leave me alone!"

"Goodbye. Be well."

The cocoon of light around Hanabi rose toward the sky, floating away from the imperial capital.

"Hero! Hero! Herooo!"

She yelled until her voice grew hoarse, but her cries didn't reach him. The Hero never looked back.

Hanabi was picked up by an escape ship. One of the few ships that managed to evacuate the city had taken little Hanabi in. Even on the ship, she just stared out the window, watching the place where she'd left Hachishiki.

The massive black moon grew further and further away...

Okegawa Kuon was at his wits' end.

The instant Hanabi had seen the fake eclipse, all trace of her regal Warrior Princess persona vanished. She began wailing like a little kid, screaming, "No!" and, "Stop!" She clung to Kuon's body, begging him not to leave her alone, not to go.

"Kuon-sama!" En yelled, appearing out of nowhere.

"En, help!"

"No, you must be the one to help her, Kuon-sama. I believe Hanabi-sama is suffering from PTSD. Start by helping her calm down."

"H-how?!"

"Talk to her. Remind her that you're here with her. Tell her she's safe, that you won't leave her alone."

Hesitantly, Kuon nodded. "S-Senpai! Hanabi-senpai! Hanabi-senpai! Don't worry! I'm right here! I'm not going any-where! I'm not leaving you! I would never leave you!"

He repeated those words over and over. Hanabi's ragged breathing gradually slowed. Her sobs stopped, and her grip on him loosened. Just before she passed out into a deep sleep, she whispered into Kuon's ear:

"Don't leave me, Hero."

As Kuon heard these words, he realized something, at long last.

She's the little girl. The last one Suzuka Hachishiki... I saved.

Hanabi slept through the rescue team's arrival and the board-ing of the Mobile Mothership *Kuou*. She was then taken to the medical room.

The other three sat in heavy silence in the tiny room where the Fuji Squad had been assigned. Tsukuba and the other senpai Cavalleria had stopped by to apologize, but the squad barely registered them.

"About Hanabi..." Rin began. "She used to do that more often. It's been a few years since her last panic attack, so I wasn't worried about it...but adrift like that, she must have gotten frightened, and it all came flooding back. I should have warned you about it. Sorry."

"No...it was careless of me..."

"Don't," Rin said, smiling. "She's always felt better once she's gotten some sleep."

"Right..." Rin's words made Kuon feel a little better. He made up his mind to ask, "Rin-san, tell me the truth about Hanabi-senpai, and what's happened since she came to Jogen." The girl he'd once saved, the girl he'd left behind... How had her life gone?

Rin hesitated at first, then sighed and began talking.

"Hanabi... Well, she survived the final battle for the capital, and was brought to Jogen. My family, Motegi—we're kind of a big name. Since she had no living relatives, we took her in, and the two of us grew up together. She was supposed to become a Motegi, too, but apparently Hanabi's folks were relatives of the Hero. My father told her, 'If the Hero saved you, you should inherit his name,' which is why she's still Suzuka. Hanabi says he was a distant relative of some sort, but the Hero had no idea they were related."

He certainly didn't. He'd had almost nothing to do with any other Suzuka after being placed in the orphanage.

"At first we fought a lot," Rin said, reminiscing. "We didn't get along at all. The shock of that war was still with Hanabi, and she didn't talk much. No matter what I said to her, it felt like she was ignoring me, and I didn't like that.

"But Hanabi's strong. If I was mean, she'd be mean right back. If I hit her, she'd hit me back, too. I was always the one who ended up crying. She'd just stare me down, not saying a word. Heheh, she was so scary.

"And she's a real try-hard. My father made us learn all sorts of things, but, even when I lost interest, Hanabi kept going. As a result, she's become way more of a proper little lady than me. You can tell, right? Even as a kid, I knew she was something special. I went back to the lessons I'd quit. But Hanabi was better at all of them, so I quit most of them again. The one I enjoyed the most and kept doing was shooting. That's the only thing I was ever better at than her.

"Slowly, the two of us grew closer. We began doing everything together. Hanabi began talking again—in a weird way, but talking—then, one day, she had her first panic attack."

Rin stared at her hands a moment. "It really rattled me. Out of nowhere, she burst into tears, threw her arms around me and began screaming, begging me not to go, not to leave her. My father later told me it was a symptom of PTSD, even though I didn't know what that meant back then. But I knew one thing right away: I knew she was seeing something I couldn't see. Something I had no way of ever seeing myself."

One of the squad members let out a long breath.

"I thought, *I've got to protect her.* I was two whole months older than her, and the eldest child of the Motegi family. Maybe she was better than me at everything, but I could be a pillow for her to hug when she needed one. Hanabi used to be all skin and bones, but she softened up considerably and grew those humongous knockers."

"That would have been a beautiful speech if it weren't for that last line," Fuji sighed, pressing his finger to his brow.

Rin carried on, unconcerned. "Hanabi chose to become a Cavalleria. She says she's doing it because she admires the Hero, but I don't think it's that simple. He certainly saved her life, but he also abandoned her. He didn't listen to her request."

That hit Kuon where it hurt. "Did she tell you what that request was?" he asked.

Rin shook her head. "She won't say. That's the only part she's never told me."

"I see..."

Take me with you! I want to die with them!

How could she say that to anyone who cared about her this much?

What if... Kuon thought. *What if part of Hanabi still wanted that? What if, like Suzuka Hachishiki in my previous life, Hanabi had a suicidal desire for a glorious death?*

She didn't seem like it; he didn't want to believe that. But could he really say for sure?

"Hanabi was a Division 5 and got into Jogen Academy with top scores—oh, I was third, and second was this guy."

"Don't jerk your thumb at me," Fuji said, brushing her hand away.

"All three of us got chosen for the Lunatic Order. We were in different squads at first. But our first year of high school, Fuji-kun formed a new squad, and we've all been together ever since. It was rough going at first, though."

Fuji nodded. "They wouldn't let us form a new squad unless we could fight and win against all seven existing squads within a set time limit. Hanabi was the key to that, but if we hadn't done something about her tendency to charge in, we'd never have managed it."

"And I'm the one who drilled proper strategy into her," said Rin.

"Well...I suppose...in a matter of speaking."

"Such enthusiasm."

"Mm. Well, we all worked hard."

Fuji's evasive wrap-up earned him a karate chop, which he blocked. Then he bowed his head at Kuon. "I'm sorry we didn't tell you sooner. Both about Suzuka-kun, and the truth about Jogen and the Imperial HQ. Let me apologize."

"N-no, it's..."

"It wasn't that we didn't trust you. We left the decision up to Suzuka-kun. We thought she understood you more than the two of us did. I hope we haven't hurt you."

"No, it's okay, I'm fine. I actually kinda feel like I forced it out of you... But, Squad Leader Fuji, Rin-kun, there is one thing I want to know."

"What is it?"

"Personally," Rin said, "I wanna know why you never call *me* 'senpai.' But what's your question?"

"You said Hanabi-senpai looks up to the Hero. And that she had a tendency to charge in."

"Mm."

"Are you at all concerned that that's because Hanabi-senpai is living too fast?"

"Living..."

"...too fast?" Fuji finished for her.

"Maybe that's a weird way to put it. But...acting like the Hero... could mean she has a death wish."

"Hmm... I've never gotten that vibe from her. Have you, Motegi-kun?"

"Yeah...I don't think so, no," Rin said. "But if you're worried about it, I think it's best to ask her."

"Like, directly?"

"But honestly, I think both 'acting like the Hero' and 'death wish' describe you more than they do her. You scare me sometimes."

"Erp. B-but I'm trying not to charge in..."

"I've got to agree. I worried about Hanabi-kun, but, watching from the back, you scare me way more than her. Starting with how you learned to move like that as a Division 1."

"Oof. Sorry."

"But again, talk to Hanabi about this. You're both Attackers. I think it'll be more productive," Rin said, fluttering her fingers.

Kuon thought he'd rid himself of Suzuka Hachishiki's bad habits, but, clearly, it didn't look that way.

While he was sulking about that, the *Kuou* made it home. By the time they reached Jogen, Hanabi had woken up.

They had six and a half years before the Queen would revive.

_/////////⌐

Everything has its limits.

The disaster had demolished Kuon's DM, but, in truth, that was the result of it not being able to keep up with him. He'd been asking too much of it for a while.

The DM Kuon had been wearing, Soukyu (Mod), had always been a beginner frame with a dirty hack of a tune-up job on top. The core design wasn't at all intended to survive Shichisei Kenbu movements, mock battles, deep sea combat, or being swallowed by the Magnetic Stream.

Basically, it was like a really kitted-out kid's tricycle. No matter how much you modded it, you couldn't climb a mountain on a tricycle.

"But you can't ride a bicycle. So we at least need to make a tricycle built for you."

Kuon was in the headmaster's office, his tiny master puffing up her large chest as she spoke.

"I think that's gonna be plenty tough..." Kuon began.

"Sword. Swi—"

"I didn't say a word!"

He was about to be reminded as to why her standards were so high.

"Don't worry. You've been riding a child's tricycle, and now you'll get a grown-up one."

What's the difference? Kuon thought.

"You try hard enough, you'll even beat a motorcycle."

"Of all the muscle-brained..."

"Sword—"

"Sorry!" Kuon apologized quickly.

"You can say what you like, but it's been in development since before you even started here."

"It has?"

"Of course, you idiot. You can't make a DM in five weeks."

He was genuinely impressed. "Master...thank you so much..."

"If you start fawning over me, I'll kill you."

"Got it!"

"Point is, Lunatic Order mock battles are temporarily suspended. You already had the next three lined up, so take a break after those. We'll need your help developing the new frame. Also, you're going to be training."

"Training?"

"With no DM, classes are a waste of time. For the month after the mock battles are over, you're camping out at my cram school training grounds."

"Okayyy..."

"I think it's still too soon, but we're outta time. If that operation goes as rumored, we've gotta get you ready."

For what? Kuon stopped himself from asking. His master looked unusually grim.

"I'm gonna teach you *all* of Shichisei Kenbu."

Which meant...

"So don't die."

...Kuon was about to reach the realm Suzuka Hachishiki never had. He was about to learn Shichisei Kenbu's ultimate arts.

"As for that, Kuon, you need to remember: In your last life, why and how did Suzuka Hachishiki die?"

"How I died...?"

"That's where it starts," she said meaningfully. There was a sad look in her eyes.

Thirteen years ago, before he'd been reborn...

Kuon would have to remember Suzuka Hachishiki's final battle.

_//////////⌐

But the times were moving faster than Nanahoshi Kaede expected.

The military were understandably skeptical about Nanahoshi Kaede's report that the Queen would return; the basis for it was flimsy at best. As a result, the Imperial Air Force were moving at odds with Kaede and Kuon's plans.

The very next day, the Imperial Air Force, Lunar Defense Force High Command put Operation Capital Fall into action.

The plan involved sending the Mobile Mothership *Kuou* into orbit, then dropping a huge number of DMs on the capital,

suppressing the enemy there. The dark mist that surrounded the capital and repelled mankind was thinner from above.

With the Operation activated, the Fuji Squad was ordered to the *Kuou*. Their orders were to be on board in three weeks.

Kuon's new frame would be completed in a month.

It would be a week too late.

Kuon wouldn't have a DM in time for the Operation.

INTERMISSION: HANABI'S DIARY 5 \\\\\\

Imperial Era 356. July 20th. Suzuka Hanabi.

I'm in love with him. I can't deny it any longer.

UNOFFICIAL RECORDS

Imperial Air Force: Assault Reconnaissance Unit. Today's MIA Count: 20.

Attempts to destroy the Gate control devices, the Flesh Pillars, have failed.

Necessity of deploying a Division 5 confirmed.

T HE NEXT DAY, in a house not far from the academy, Okegawa Kuon sat in his room, staring at his desk.

"This is *really* embarrassing..." Kuon muttered. More specifically, he was staring at a beautifully bound book on his desk.

The title on the cover read *Portrait of the Hero*.

I never dreamed I'd have a book written about me.

Trying to recover the memories of his previous life, he'd borrowed Suzuka Hachishiki's biography from Hanabi. It wasn't like he'd forgotten or anything, but it had been thirteen years ago. It couldn't hurt to have some documentation.

Hanabi must have read this book so much. The cover was worn but had clearly been well-looked after. Having a total stranger write about his life, and having that special female senpai read it was...well, really embarrassing.

But this was for the ultimate arts. He had to do it.

Gritting his teeth, Kuon opened the book.

"Oh. Yeah, that's right."

Okegawa Kuon's memories came flooding back to him.

These are the final memories of the Cavalleria who killed more Jave than any other human.

Once, there was a man named Suzuka Hachishiki, a.k.a. the Hero.

He was a Maneuver Cavalleria, Squad Leader of the Imperial Air Force, City Defense Force, First Mobile Division, Suzuka Squad.

He'd been deployed to mop up the Gate that had suddenly appeared over the imperial capital, as well as any Jave coming through it. He and his companions flew out to the battlefield, but along the way he'd lost all his companions in combat with monsters from another world. He alone reached the airspace over the capital.

"Let's go, Getsuei (8-Phase)!" Calling the name of his beloved frame, the Hero flew alone into the thick of battle.

Falling to the surface, Hachishiki looked down at the black shadows writhing everywhere. It was an entire swarm of the human race's natural predator.

The dark purple swarm filled his vision. Monsters that looked like defective disks covered in writhing tentacles waited to swallow Hachishiki as he fell. Just one of these would be a tough target for three normal Maneuver Cavalleria.

But Hachishiki showed no fear. He merely readied the large rifle in his right hand. His visor showed his altitude and speed, radar information like enemy and ally positions, and everything else he needed to know to fight effectively. In the center were his sights, showing "Locked On" and "Charge Ready."

There was no reason to hesitate. There was nothing on his radar but enemies.

The instant he pulled the trigger, a Jave several meters long was swallowed by blinding light. Hachishiki had fired his Scout Nova Rifle, a weapon that was more powerful the stronger the wielder's magic was. The "Nova" it fired was magic transformed to an ultra-heated beam of light, which traveled at the speed of light. It vaporized the tentacle monster, striking the surface below.

A shock wave spread out from the impact center. The ground shook. The dark purple swarm pulsed outward like a crowd doing the wave at a soccer match.

An instant later, there was a massive explosion.

Hachishiki was at 800 meters now, and the pillar of fire just barely missed hitting him. This was followed by a rush of noise, a billow of black smoke, and the distinctive scent of a magical beam explosion. The 265 Jave on the surface were vaporized instantly... along with the town below them.

To be clear, there were no signs of any non-Jave biological response—no humans were left alive.

The DM detection ability was never wrong. While Hachishiki was on his way there, the citizenry had been squashed under buildings, burned to death, or eaten by the monsters, along with their dogs and cats.

Despite unleashing a blast that would have put anyone else in a week-long magic depletion coma, Hachishiki was still fighting. His nozzles fired, slowing his descent, and he hovered above the surface, looking around.

There was a swarm of flying Jave headed his way. There wasn't much difference between them and the ones he'd just vaporized. While the surface Jave were disk-like, the flying ones were like opened fans or hideous, malformed manta rays swimming through the air. He had only one thing for them:

Extermination.

He pointed his Scout Nova Rifle at the center of the swarm and they responded. They split into two groups, swinging to the left and right to try attacking from both sides. Were they actually strategizing? Or was that just instinct?

Hachishiki didn't care. He just fired, starting with the group on the right.

There was another explosion like a sun being born upon the surface. The clouds being blown away showed the progress of the shockwave. One of the two groups was completely gone. Meanwhile, the other doubled its speed, coming closer. *Ah ha, the first had been bait.* They planned to end this before his rifle could recharge. Not a bad plan for a pack of monsters.

The tips of every manta began glowing. It was an incredible number of lights, like looking at the stars in the sky. His visor sounded an alert as the enemy attacked with their invisible bullets—132 of them.

Shichisei Kenbu: Tensetsu.

Saying the name of the technique aloud helped focus the

mind. The effect took hold. In that instant, Hachishiki's senses crossed the dimensional barrier, and it felt like time around him had stopped. In a negative-image world, the bullets appeared frozen in the air.

He could see how to evade them. If any of this rain of bullets hit him, he'd die instantly, but he saw several lines that would allow him to escape unharmed.

Time moved again.

His body moved faster than thought. It felt less like he was dodging than the bullets just missed on their own. He simply flew forward, following the line. Passing through their attack, he found the Jave swarm right in front of him, almost moving at the speed of sound.

By this point, the back of Hachishiki's frame already had eight symmetrical armaments deployed. He grabbed the one to the upper right; the hilt bore the old kanji for "one," *ichi*. He drew the pitch-black Blade that was charged with his magic.

Shichisei Kenbu: Ryusui.

The first wave of Jave flew by. The eight mantas in the first formation let out a horrible scream, their bodies falling to pieces. Black Jave blood turned to mist, scattering everywhere. As they'd passed Hachishiki, he'd cut them apart.

He grabbed the "nana" Blade from his upper left and breathed out. "That all you got?"

Enemies rushed at him from the front, left and right, above and below. He stopped time with Tensetsu, found a path, and used his two swords to turn the monsters into sashimi.

On a battlefield with no other survivors, a single Cavalleria was dominating the monsters from another world.

Hachishiki's Blades stopped only when he'd dismembered the last of the fliers. The sky around him was dark, like it was covered in storm clouds. Jave blood filled the air like mist, corrupting the atmosphere.

The radar showed a second and third wave of enemies approaching. He had seventy-five seconds before they were in range. He could normally handle them, but not this time. He'd exterminated the enemies here, and there were no humans left alive, so there was no harm in abandoning this place to the Jave.

But he wasn't retreating. He ignored the approaching waves and headed for the Gate.

Forty-five percent magic remaining. He took a small box from the item pack on his frame, removed a pill, and popped it in his mouth. His vision narrowed, turning red, his heart racing. These were hardly good for him, but they effectively restored his magic instantaneously. By the time his breathing recovered, he was fully charged. He'd likely carved three years off his life span, but who cared? He was dying today.

"But before I do, I've got to crush this Gate."

No one had succeeded in taking out a Gate yet. If it went well, it would aid the generation to come.

With one glance back at the approaching mantas, Hachishiki's Getsuei (8-Phase) flew off toward the heart of the capital.

Hachishiki's final destination was the Gate over the imperial capital, Tokyo. His final goal was to destroy the Gate, dying in the process.

Suzuka Hachishiki wanted to die, to go out in a blaze of glory.

He didn't want to be alone anymore. He didn't want to be left behind anymore. That's why he wanted to die while taking as many Jave as possible with him.

Then, he met the little girl.

"They... They're all dead! Please! I want to die with them! I want to go where they are!"

He'd saved her, but Hachishiki couldn't grant her request.

He was genuinely sorry; he felt it was selfish of him. But he wanted this child he'd only just met and barely knew to live, if only to lend that much more meaning to his own death. Even though she felt the same way he did.

Her eyes looked just like his had when he was young, and he couldn't bear it.

_//////////

A black force field, like a black hole, swirled in the sky over the heart of the capital. It was 300 meters across, but only a centimeter thick. This was the Gate connecting the Jave's world to this one.

There were four giant flesh pillars placed around it. These were believed to be control panels, and Hachishiki destroyed all four as soon as he arrived. The instant the fourth pillar collapsed, the Gate opened.

A chill ran over him. His instincts screamed at him to pull back.

Tensetsu showed all evasion routes leading directly backward. He ignored them all, standing his ground. Suzuka Hachishiki wasn't retreating today.

A massive Jave appeared from beyond the dimensional barrier, one almost as large as the Gate itself. It was disk-shaped, like the surface Jave, but instead of that dark purple it was a shade of red that reminded him of internal organs. He'd never seen this type before; it was a total unknown. It had mouths all over it, which yawned open, spewing countless flying Jave.

Hachishiki knew then this was the Queen.

His lips twisted into a smile. His Scout Nova Rifle fired instantly.

The mantas served as the Queen's shield. A massive fireball appeared between the Queen and Hachishiki, but that was all. The rifle that had extinguished hundreds of Jave couldn't even reach the Queen.

Light gathered in front of the Queen as she prepared to re-turn fire. Jave bullets were normally invisible, but the sheer heat index made this one visible to the naked eye.

A strange sense of elation filled Hachishiki's heart. He tossed his rifle aside and drew the last of his Blades, Hachi.

He would show her his strongest art.

Shichisei Kenbu: Shijin Reppakuzan.

It felt like his entire body was on fire. The DM amplified his magic several times over, and Getsuei (8-Phase) couldn't keep up with the shimmer of heat surrounding it. Several mantas came flying in but were evaporated before they reached him. Humanity's most powerful magic was fully unleashed, and all of it was channeled into a single Blade. Hachishiki raised the Blade far above his head.

The Queen attacked first, firing her beam, but...

"Shijin!" Hachishiki screamed. "Reppakuzan!"

He swung, his sword a blade of red light that seemed to stretch as far as the sky itself.

The Queen's bullet was every bit as powerful as the Scout Nova Rifle's Nova, but it was swallowed up by the infinitely long red blade. The sword reached the Queen, attempting to slice that massive mound of flesh in twain.

Skreeeeeeeeeeeeeeeeeeeeeeeeeeeeeeeeeeeeeeeeeeeeeeeeeeee!

The Jave Queen let out a scream that shook the Earth itself. The noise sent a wave of sickness rising from within, scraping away at his very mind. Hachishiki grit his teeth, releasing all the magic he'd put into the sword.

"Break!"

Everything within a kilometer was instantly vaporized by an explosion several times larger than the light. Abandoned office buildings, apartment complexes, hospitals, houses, parks, bridges, the Jave eggs laid in all of those—everything was blown away. The shockwave was like a tornado, followed by a second rush of wind as the atmosphere raced to fill the vacuum created at the heart of the explosion. The black mist, which was all that remained of the Jave, turned into a giant whirlpool at the heart of the crater.

Everything was swept away except for two things: Suzuka Hachishiki, and the Gate itself.

"Still hanging in there, huh?"

He was breathing heavily. He popped another magic recovery pill. He'd been told to wait at least three days between them, but what did it matter? For a moment, his heart stopped beating. His vision went black. All sound drained away. He felt himself falling, but quickly recovered his balance. He'd overdosed on the pills. Sweat poured out of him as less than half his magic came back.

It didn't matter.

He used Tensetsu and his speed to search his surroundings. Trace magic made it clear the Queen had been blown back through the Gate. The shockwave must have gotten her, throwing her back through the dimensional barrier before she vaporized.

The Hero didn't hesitate. He sent Getsuei (8-Phase) right through the Gate; he wasn't letting the Queen get away. While he was at it, if there was no way to destroy the Gate from the outside, he'd take care of it from the inside.

Hachishiki flew through the swirling vortex into another world without noticing how unbalanced his behavior was.

It was quiet.

Hachishiki floated slowly in what looked so much like the space between the Earth and the Moon. It was similar to what he'd experienced doing atmosphere re-entry tests on Fourth Generation DM prototypes, but there was neither a moon nor the Earth here.

His instruments were all out of whack. If he were to blindly trust his radar, speedometer, altimeter, and magic meter, Hachishiki was currently inside a bubble of magic with a value of 7,777,777 while traveling at three times the speed of light at an altitude of -5000 meters. He ignored them. There was something else he needed to look for first.

The Jave Queen was floating at five o'clock. Two-thirds of the Queen had vanished, and there was a glowing purple Core-like thing exposed. She was touching this with her tentacles, as if trying to heal.

He knew instinctively that he had to smash the Core.

He fired up every nozzle on his back, charging forward. His head was screaming in pain. *Shut up,* he told it. *We don't have long left anyway. There's no way back to our world, so let's take as many Jave with us as we can.*

This last thought was basically his motto. Once again, it burned a path across his mind. If the Queen recovered and went back through the Gate, there were no humans left who stood a chance against her. This wasn't over-confidence or bragging—it was the sad and simple truth.

Fortunately, his Blade was intact. He couldn't use any major arts, but all he had to do was hit home once. As he flew into the enemy's range, at the back of his mind he thought, *I can still move, even here.* Then he realized his radar was still active. It was displaying enemy coordinates with precision. The alarms were sounding. A moment later, countless spear-like tentacles shot out of empty space. He activated Tensetsu semi-unconsciously. As time froze, he looked for a way to evade.

There wasn't one.

"At last…"

His body was run through. He coughed up blood.

His consciousness began fading. His body was on fire. The pain was beating an anvil in his head. The tentacles were still inside him, slowly pulling him apart. He was so close he could almost touch the Queen's Core…

Then it moved.

Inside the glowing purple light of the Fore, there was a thin, dark fissure, like an eye. A bottomless, murky pupil. The heart of this filthy ball of flesh that thought it had won.

Heh…heheh…heheheh…

He tried laughing out loud, but he couldn't move his mouth. He laughed in his mind instead as he spat one last clichéd insult at the invader.

You goddamn ugly monster.

He'd always wanted to try it, to go out in a blaze of glory, but the moment had never been right. *At last,* he thought. Now he could finally use it—the final self-destruct art.

Shichisei Kenbu: Soryu Ranbu.

The DM's alarm fell silent. There was no need to warn him anymore. When he used Soryu Ranbu, he gathered magic, contracting and compressing it within his frame, consciously forcing it past the critical state. Maintaining control over this excessive magic was extremely difficult, but not impossible for anyone trained in Shichisei Kenbu; nor was intentionally setting it off.

Sensing he was up to something, the tentacles tried tearing Hachishiki apart, but it was too late. He surpassed the critical compression threshold and the pent-up magic scattered. This was the art named for and modeled after the ancient dragon that was the source of all magic, and the dance it performed. When Hachishiki unleashed his magic, it pulled in all the magic from around them, scattering it. Magic is the hidden potential of man, the energy of human life. That very life was torn up and scattered.

Once, there was a god who could kill things just by breathing on them. This was that very wind—the blowing breath of death known as Magic Dispersal.

The Jave Queen crumbled, falling apart. She no longer had the magic to maintain physical form.

At the heart of this slaughter, the focal point of it all, Hachishiki did not survive it either. Feeling the last embers of his mind fading, he remembered the words of the little girl...

"Hero, are you gonna die?"

Hachishiki lost consciousness then. It felt the same as his eyelids closing just before falling asleep in a darkened room.

Thus, the Hero perished.

Thirteen years passed. Reborn as Okegawa Kuon, he began his training in the ultimate arts so he could kill the Queen for good.

Yet he still didn't understand what his master's words about the Hero's death had meant.

DIVISIONMANEUVER

CHAPTER 6

The Hero Ardent

THE FUJI SQUAD had twenty days until they were due on board the *Kuou*.

Hanabi was in a deep slump. In their mock battles, Kuon used a temporary frame (a dust-covered Division 1 frame found in storage) and his and Hanabi's routine was off, screwing up their combo. Hanabi had accidentally shot Kuon three times in a row.

Because of this, the Fuji Squad were now ranked second. Kuon was pulled away from the squad for training and to help adjust his new frame. The Fuji Squad had to fight rank battles with only the three of them, so it would be hard to take back the crown. There was a very good chance they would continue sliding down the rankings.

Hanabi's slump was clearly the cause of it.

Squad Leader Fuji just said, "Her attack the other day is clearly the cause. These things take time to heal."

Maybe it's the stress of this big Operation, Kuon thought.

Subleader Rin, however, knew it was neither.

Hanabi shed tears she normally never let anyone see, and apologized to the boys, who tried cheering her up.

Rin said, "Let me handle this," sent them both home, and stayed in the meeting room with Hanabi to speak privately.

"I hope Hanabi-senpai will be okay..."

"Motegi-kun's like a sister to her. Nothing to worry about," Fuji said. But then he hesitated. "Have you talked to Suzuka-kun about...you-know-what, yet?"

The death wish thing, Kuon thought. "No, I haven't had a chance... She really hasn't been talking to me at all lately. Even when I borrowed that book, she was kinda curt about it."

"Mm. It'll take a lot out of you both, I'm sure. But, Okegawa-kun, the Operation isn't going away. We're Cavalleria. So long as we live, we must be prepared for death. You know that, right?"

"Exactly. I'm worried those orders will give her the excuse she needs to go out and..." he trailed off.

"Hmph. Suzuka-kun can be direct like that. But she has her frail side, and a good man would try supporting her. I think you should be the one to bring it up."

"Yeah... Wait, are we talking about the same thing?"

"Mm? What...? Oh, sorry, I've got to go."

Fuji was looking toward the school gate at a girl Kuon didn't recognize, presumably from the high school. She was quite a beauty. *No way,* Kuon thought. But he had to ask, right? "Um, Squad Leader, is that your girlfriend?"

"No."

"Oh, then your sister?"

"No," Fuji said, shaking his head. "My fiancée."

Kuon stared at him.

"What? You look like a pigeon shot by a satellite cannon."

"I don't know if there'd be anything left of that pigeon to look at, but...fiancée?!"

"Like I said, we don't know when we're going to die. So say what you want to say while you still can."

"Still..."

"I merely suggested that if I came back alive we should get married. A fiancée won't become a widow, after all."

"You're setting up your own death flag!"

"And I'll chop it back down on my way forward. Good luck with yours," Fuji said, slapping Kuon on his shoulder. Then an idea hit him. "Since you're here, let me introduce you. Okegawa-kun, do you have a few minutes?"

"Uh, sure..." Kuon went with him.

Fuji's fiancée was neither strong-willed like Hanabi or a fun tease like Rin. She was more of a soft, comforting presence.

I guess I know why Squad Leader Fuji never hooked up with either of them...

There were all kinds of love, Kuon realized, despite having no experience with love in either of his lives.

Naturally, Rin had been aware for a while.

Hanabi had been acting weird even before she began accidentally shooting Kuon. Staring at nothing, sighing for no reason, listening to love songs she'd never listened to before... Whenever she talked to Rin, she always seemed to be looking for someone and was very concerned about her text notifications. She'd even swapped out the hair tie on her ponytail for a cute ribbon.

"So, Hanabi."

Once the boys had left, Rin locked the door to the meeting room, deployed her DM despite the rules against using them indoors, used the frame's radar to make a thorough check for open comms or bugs, then released the DM and sat down opposite Hanabi, their knees almost touching.

"Just to be absolutely sure."

"Mmm..."

Hanabi was in full maiden mode, acting quite demure, possibly meek, or maybe just depressed.

"Your slump isn't caused by the attack or the pressure from the Operation."

"No..."

Rin sighed, half relieved, half annoyed. There could only be one other reason. Rin glanced at the door over Hanabi's shoulder and said, very deliberately, "Oh, Kyuu-kun, what is it?"

"Eeek!" Hanabi shrieked with surprise, her head snapping around like she was trying to do a full 180-degree turn.

There was nobody there.

Hanabi's head snapped back, glaring at Rin, her face bright red. Rin sighed again, not the least bit guilty. "You are way too into Kyuu-kun."

Hanabi groaned. Then she tried to explain. "But... But how can I not be?"

"I knew from the start you liked Kyuu-kun, but it wasn't this bad, was it?"

"You knew?!"

"It was obvious."

Hanabi groaned again. "When... When he joined our squad, at first I was just happy. But..."

"But?"

"But slowly I lost control of my feelings. Then the attack came. I ended up clinging to him while he said he'd be with me and never leave me, over and over, like the real Hero was comforting me and... I just can't. I can't even look at him. Ever. You get it, Rin? During Tensetsu we're staring at each other the whole time! Everyone's senses are frozen and only Kuon-kun and I are conscious, staring at each other! I can't do that! I can't look at him, so I can't tell what everyone's evasion routes are, but then I look at Kuon-kun and accidentally fire... Right now just saying 'Kuon-kun' out loud is enough to make my heart ready to burst."

Rin had clearly reached her limit. She went over to the window, flung it open, and screamed, "What is this, a shoujo mangaaaaaaaaaaaaaaaaaaa?!"

Before the echoes had died down, she spun around, pointing at Hanabi. "Tell him!"

Hanabi went even redder, tears in her eyes. "I-I can't... I can't do that!"

This was so cute it really got to Rin. "Then go on a date!"

"A d-d-d-date?! Never! Absolutely impossible!"

"Yeah, I knew that. Tell you what: You have Kyuu-kun teaching you Fencing, right?"

"Y-yeah."

"And you've shot Kyuu-kun three times in mock battles with your rifle."

"Aughhh...."

"Don't start crying! You need to thank him for the lessons and apologize for shooting him! To do that, you're gonna take a whole day off and take Kyuu-kun around wherever he likes, and treat him to some great food! You've got the Cavalleria reward money, right?"

"I've never spent any of it..."

Never? Rin thought, exasperated. "Then use it now to demonstrate your gratitude!"

"My gratitude... I do want say thank you...and sorry..."

"If you think about it that way, you can totally do it, right? It won't be a date. Just paying back a debt."

"Not a date, just a thank you," Hanabi said, considering it. "Got it. I'll do it! You're always such a help, Rin."

"Don't worry about it. And I gotta apologize while I'm at it. Sorry, Hanabi. I told him about your panic attacks."

"O-oh. No, you were right to. I should have told him myself."

"Then you just need to make Kyuu-kun hug you. I'm not gonna let you hug me anymore."

"O-oh no! Don't abandon me, Rin!"

"Don't look at me like that!" Rin told her. "Okay, okay...I can see where this is heading."

"Oh, by the way, Rin."

"What?"

"What does 'www' mean? In my diary..."

"World Wide Web."

"I knew it!" Hanabi exclaimed.

"Yup."

"But then underneath it, it said 'Liar' and some more Ws."

"No, I deleted that part—ack!" Rin had let it slip.

"I knew it was you!" Hanabi shouted.

"Oops," Rin apologized.

Hanabi's well-toned biceps unleashed a powerful karate chop on Rin's clearly guilty head. Rin bit her tongue and wound up curled up in the corner of the room, clutching her mouth. Hanabi felt ever so slightly guilty; perhaps she'd overdone it.

But a minute later she remembered that Rin had read her super embarrassing diary and gave Rin another karate chop before going to the opposite corner and dying of mortification.

_//////////⌐

Kuon's training was brutal.

One art in Shichisei Kenbu was called Shimetsu. It was the art he'd used to negate Hanabi's maximized Nova during the entrance ceremony. The art involved pinpointing the core of a light bullet and destroying it to render the shot ineffective, and the ultimate art Kuon was learning was an extension of this.

"Shimetsu shows you the core of a light bullet, but the ultimate art takes that even further, showing you the core of magic itself. Magic is the hidden power all humans have, their life essence. In other words..."

Kaede's voice came from above. Kuon was laying like a heap of rags by the river bank near the training grounds.

"...magic is the light of life. Before anything else, you need to be able to see that in Tensetsu. So—hey, are you listening? You're still alive, aren't you?"

"Yes..."

"Good. Ten-minute rest. Then I'll drop you back in that river—and, of course, that blindfold and those handcuffs and shackles are staying on. You will remain on standby down there for two hours. I will, of course, allow DM activation, but if you don't manage your magic properly you'll run out along the way. The DM will release, and you'll drown, so be careful. Unless you like sleeping with the fishes."

Since ancient times, practicing in water had been a traditional way of intensifying training. Shichisei Kenbu came from a long tradition and was no exception. Later on, Kuon would be escorted to the mountains and forced to train with less oxygen, but he had no way of knowing that, and Kaede wasn't about to tell him. It might break his will.

There were risks involved with this intense training: hypothermia and suffocation in the water, hemorrhaging from altitude sickness, and oxygen deprivation in the mountains. Because these risks could prove fatal, Kuon slowly began grasping the first step toward learning the ultimate arts—the breathing method that would dramatically throttle his magic expenditure.

But...

It's still not enough.

As she threw a bound and shackled thirteen-year-old in the river, Kaede's expression grew grim.

Kuon did not surface.

It was the day before the Fuji Squad was due on board the *Kuou*. Kuon had learned all too well the mental toll of being dropped in a river while blindfolded and bound, unable to see or move. The only thing that kept him sane was En chattering away at him, but...

"Good Morning, Jogen! It's the start of the happy hour, ready to blow all your Monday blues away! This is DJ NSR's mega-cool, hyperactive super radio show, Repsol 999!

"Enjoy without fear of leaking water! Okay, first song coming up, Ifukube Akio's 'Kenjutsu Shobai'! *Hmm hmmhmmm hmmm*!" She then hummed the entire number.

Without En's wackiness, he genuinely would have been in trouble. If he counted all the times in the last three weeks Kaede and this inane humming radio show had made his urge to kill rise, he'd be in the three digits. The way Kaede met his fury head on, never once ceasing her torment, and the way En happily kept the broadcast going were both impressive in their own ways.

Kuon still had enough left in him to be impressed.

The rest of the Fuji Squad (without Kuon) would board the Mobile Battleship *Kuou* tomorrow. After that, they would be on standby until the Operation began, so they had less than thirty hours of free time remaining.

That morning was the first day off he'd been granted since his training began, and he spent it catching up on sleep. He slept like the dead. The last ten days he'd managed only twenty hours of sleep total; even he was amazed he'd survived it.

But as he slept too deeply to even dream, the Device by his pillow rang. Rubbing his eyes, he glanced at the window, trying to focus on the name displayed:

Suzuka Hanabi-senpai.

This is a date.
No, it isn't, it's "thanks" and "sorry," an expression of my gratitude. But also a date.
No, no, it's not. Definitely not. Thanks. Sorry. And...

These thoughts ran through Hanabi's head on a loop. She sat alone at the largest shopping district on Jogen, waiting for Kuon.

They'd agreed to meet there. That much was definitively true, date or not.

Hanabi had made Rin triple-check her outfit but was still worried it was weird. She didn't know how to hold her expensive-looking purse and she felt like the front of her shirt was open a little too far down and sure, it was always summer on the island but going entirely sleeveless was dubious and this skirt was definitely too short. She was getting so many glances from passersby that were fanning her anxiety. She should have just worn her uniform, although Rin would have stopped her if she'd left in a track suit.

Hanabi and Kuon had agreed to meet under a giant clock. "It's cliché, but... No, it's easily understood, which I think is for the best," Rin had said when she suggested it. But that meant Rin also knew where they were meeting. That was obvious, but Hanabi was way too stressed about her first date *(no, my expression of gratitude)* to realize what that meant.

Ding, dong, ding.

The bell rang. It was exactly noon.

Kuon wasn't there.

She began fretting. Maybe he wasn't coming. Kuon said he'd been training to master the ultimate arts this whole time. When she'd called him that morning, he'd just woken up. Maybe he was so tired he fell back asleep? Or was his promise to her just not as important? After all, they were the Shichisei Kenbu ultimate arts. In a DM, he'd be humanity's strongest swordsman. It didn't take three seconds to know which was more important: her or those arts.

A lump formed in Hanabi's chest. The anxious lump grew bigger and bigger until she could barely breathe. She felt so ashamed for getting all excited about this, for trying to dress up in the sort of thing she never wore. She felt so pathetic, but she couldn't let herself cry. She should just leave. *Just wait five more minutes. No, three. And if he doesn't come...*

"Sorry to keep you waiting, Hanabi-senpai!"

He's here.

Kuon was right in front of her. She'd been staring at her hands and hadn't noticed him coming.

He was apologizing, looking all flustered. "I'm sorry! You

looked so beautiful I thought you were a model or something. I just walked right past you, not even realizing it was you. Only after looking everywhere else—"

"You came."

She must have looked incredibly happy. "Yes. Um, senpai," Kuon said, fidgeting. He looked embarrassed. "You look really lovely."

Hanabi stared at her hands again.

Meanwhile, both Rin and En threw their thumbs up.

En, always by Kuon's side, was naturally in "Sleep Mode" and not visible, yet still feeding Rin a detailed account. Actually, she'd gotten lazy halfway through and just started broadcasting a live feed directly over the link to Rin.

But...

Damn you, Hanabi... You aren't talking to Kyuu-kun at all! What's so fascinating about the ground?! You aren't supposed to be staring at the sandals I loaned you, you're supposed to be looking at the boy next to you!

Rin was watching them from the shadows through the PGM-F4 Rifle Scope she used for shooting practice, and she was furious to see Hanabi with her head down.

A few hours later, Headmaster Nanahoshi would uncover this scheme, and both Rin and En would be sent to the brig.

The first date between the Hero Reborn and the Warrior Princess was off to a rocky start.

Officially, this was to thank him for his help while they were adrift, apologize for shooting him during mock events, and express her gratitude for his help with her Fencing. Hanabi had asked Kuon where he wanted to go, but...

"Maybe an onsen?" he'd said, looking extremely serious.

The two eavesdropping had simultaneously yelled, "What are you, a grandpa?! No thirteen-year-old would say that!"

"Oh, sorry, no onsen in the shopping district!" Hanabi said. "Let's try a sento instead!"

Not the point.

Not the problem, either.

A girl and an AI tightened their firsts, desperate to communicate their feelings. Sure, there was a sento here, but...

Meanwhile, Hanabi was quickly realizing the suggestions Rin had given her for this date were going to be of no use at all. At a loss, she blurted out, "There's a really big bath at the Motegi house. I could wash your back there?" Then she had a mental image of herself in the bath with Kuon, both of them naked, and her about to touch his back. She hastily yelped, "No, never mind!"

They both wound up turning red. They were hopeless.

"Um... Then is there anything else you'd like?" Hanabi asked, trying to recover.

"Um...some chocolate? You know how it was back on the mainland. The shops were all closed."

"O-okay!" Hanabi cheered up immediately. This was on Rin's list.

Rin was too busy gloating in the shadows to notice the suspicious looks she was engendering.

"There's a shop that imports chocolate from overseas. Let's go there, Kuon-kun!"

"Okay!"

It went smoothly after that.

The Jave had ruined many sea lanes, making chocolate a highly sought-after and expensive commodity, but when Kuon balked at the price, Hanabi essentially forced him to let her buy him some. She was struck by how nice the shop clerk was being.

After that they really did go to a sento, soaked for a while, then sat side-by-side on the massage chairs between all the senior citizens.

"Ahhh..."

Kuon caught a whiff of that post-bath smell from Hanabi, and when her yukata parted slightly, and he caught a glimpse of cleavage, or found his eyes automatically drawn to her long legs and arms in the one-size-fits-all yukata, he forced himself not to look. But he couldn't help stealing glances. She really did have big boobs. They were as big as his face. Remembering how he'd had his face stuck in the valley between them in the deep sea, he was forced to shake his head to rid himself of those thoughts.

After a lengthy sequence of such glances and head shakes, the old lady next to him said, "Good luck out there," and gave him some candy. Confused, he looked from her face to the candy in his palm. "You're Cavalleria, right?" she said, smiling. "I used to live on the mainland, you know." Only now did he realize why the chocolatier clerk had been so nice. He was still only in his first year at the Cavalleria school, and not used to this treatment. It was a good reminder that he was fighting to protect these people.

They'd both done quite well.

Kuon helped ease Hanabi's stress about the summons tomorrow, and Hanabi helped relieve the physical and mental exhaustion Kuon had built up.

Neither of them put what they most wanted to say into words, but the time flew by, and they had so much fun.

At the end of the "date," they stood together at the bus stop, waiting for the bus to go home. Hanabi would be going back to the dorm, and Kuon to the training grounds.

This was goodbye.

At this time of day, not many people used the bus line leading from the shopping district to the academy. The hologram bus schedule had a forlorn glow to it as Kuon and Hanabi stared at it in silence.

Hanabi was reminded again, as she had been all day, that she really enjoyed Kuon's company, and that his smile brought her joy. She'd already put it into words in her diary, and she'd spent the whole day thinking that same thought over and over.

Fuji had said what he had to say to his fiancée, and while Rin had no such partner, Hanabi knew she never would have hesitated to express her feelings.

Hanabi knew she was being weak, and she knew she couldn't

let herself be that way. She may never come back. She would be dropped on the capital, and there was every chance she'd never come back to Jogen.

She may never see him again.

"Kuon-kun."

She looked at him. He was so short. So thin, yet well-built, with muscles where he needed them. He had strong-willed, confident eyes. A demeanor so calm it was hard to believe he was five years younger than her, were it not for the occasional moment of childishness. And those tough little hands that spoke of how hard he'd worked—the hands of a swordsman.

He looked back at Hanabi, staring directly into her eyes, waiting for her words.

Say it.

Say it.

Say it now.

"I'm in...in, in, iiin..."

The bus arrived with flawless timing.

"...iiinterested to see how great a Cavalleria you'll become!"

Hanabi suddenly felt extremely tired.

Kuon smiled. "Thanks," he said. "I know you'll be a great Cavalleria, too."

"Mm, thanks." She smiled listlessly and took a step onto the bus. She wanted to die.

"Senpai!"

Kuon was looking up at her from the bus stop. There was an urgency, a grim look in his eyes.

"I'm really, really sorry I can't join you in the Operation tomorrow. Please, please..."

The bus drove away. Hanabi was the only passenger. She sat in the very back, her face buried in her hands, remembering the words he'd said as the door closed.

"Please...fight with honor."

He must have wanted to say that all day. The fact that he couldn't fight with the rest of the Fuji Squad must have gnawed at him the whole time they were together—when they were eating, in the baths, when he smiled... It didn't matter to her that he wouldn't be joining her in battle; she understood.

She must have been the only one genuinely enjoying their time together, and that made her feel absolutely terrible. She was completely ashamed of herself. The pained look on his face wouldn't leave her mind.

Don't... Don't let that be the last I see of you.

The bus drove on.

With nobody else on board, Hanabi cried softly.

"What am I even doing?!"

Watching through her scope from the next stop over, Rin thought about what Hanabi hadn't said, and what Kuon had said to Hanabi, and what both of those things meant. She suddenly felt helpless.

What was she doing, watching her friend's date like a nosy little sister?

When the bus arrived, Rin didn't get on. At the back of it,

Hanabi didn't see Rin standing there.

The bus drove away.

Kuon had said less than half of what he'd wanted to say.

He watched the bus drive off with Hanabi on board, feeling like it was taking her right into the battlefield. He'd wanted to talk with her longer and spend more time together. He wished to go into battle with her tomorrow, fight by her side till the bitter end.

Feeling empty inside, not even realizing why he was suddenly so depressed, Kuon began slowly walking away toward the training grounds.

He looked around the darkened streets. Then...

I might never see her again.

That thought struck him. It was possible. She might never...

"Kuon-sama," En said, coming out of Sleep Mode.

"Yeah?" he said, trying not to let the panic show.

"I know it's bad manners, but I did hear your last conversation."

"Oh." Weirdly, he couldn't bring himself to be mad.

En bowed, then spoke in an unusually subdued tone. "Kuon-sama, this is really something Hanabi-sama should tell you herself, so I've kept quiet about it until now. But she'll be gone tomorrow, and possibly won't be coming back, so I feel like there isn't time for that. So, while I hesitate to do so, I think I'd better be the one to tell you."

"What? Get to the point."

"That was Hanabi trying to tell you she loves you."

His brain short-circuited. "Huh? Seriously?!"

"Seriously, Kuon-sama."

"You're kidding!"

"I am not, Kuon-sama."

"But...she said I'd be a great Cavalleria!"

"She couldn't bring herself to say the word 'love.'"

"Seriously?"

"I am extremely serious, Kuon-sama. She sees you as childlike."

This was just stupid. "But I'm a mature, thirty-five-year-old man inside!"

"No, no, Kuon-sama. You are childlike in a good way, although that time when you almost got in a serious fight with Rin-sama over fried chicken...that perhaps couldn't be categorized as mature."

"I suppose it couldn't..."

"But you are a cocky little brat, in a good way."

"A cocky little brat," he repeated.

"I suspect your surroundings and your physical age have an effect."

"They do...but... En, that's how you see me?!"

"How do you intend on responding to Hanabi-sama's feelings?"

"How...? I don't..."

"Oh, now you're all flustered. I thought for sure you liked her, too."

"No, I mean, sure, maybe I'm a bit of a kid, but I'm seventeen years older than senpai. I feel like I shouldn't be messing around with anyone that young."

"You look like a total shota and you're saying that?" En demanded. "And you're still calling her 'senpai.' With respect."

"I do respect her."

"Do you think of her as a younger, beautiful high school girl or an older, beautiful lady? Which comes to mind first?"

Kuon thought about it. He supposed it was both at once. This was tricky.

"You don't love her?" En said, getting right at the heart of it. He hesitated. She didn't let up. "This is a time of war. Both of you are Cavalleria. She might die tomorrow."

"I know that."

"It's better to give your answer soon."

His answer...to the confession she'd almost managed.

"Show her your grown-up confidence, Kuon-sama. A proper man says what he means with no shame, no embarrassment, and with confidence and clarity. That's what makes women weak in the knees."

Kuon closed his eyes, raising his face to the sky. Thinking. Thinking. Thinking thinking thinking...

Thinking he didn't need to think.

He'd only said half of what he wanted to say.

He opened his eyes. There was a crescent moon in the sky, the type of moon Jogen was named after.

"En."

"Yes."

"I'm only thirteen. I don't *have* any grown-up confidence. But..."

Kuon began running in the direction the bus had gone, to where Hanabi was. As he did, Rin called him. She'd heard the whole thing from En, but Kuon was unaware of this, so, as he ran, he just listened to what she had to say.

Take care of Hanabi.

He was suddenly very glad for all the training his master had put him through. All that endurance running hadn't been for nothing.

When he reached the dorm, Hanabi was just getting off the bus.

He looked up and saw her gazing up at the moon, looking far, far lonelier than she had when they were at the bottom of the ocean together.

"Senpai."

The Jogen Academy dorm was huge, surrounded by a tall fence that seemed to go on forever. Hanabi was standing by the gate, clutching a tiny purse in both hands.

When Kuon spoke, she spun around, surprised. But her expression soon faded, her eyes narrowing.

"What? You came running after me?" Her voice had turned cold, like ice.

"Um, there was something I wanted to talk about. Are you up for a walk?"

"It's almost curfew. If you want to talk, do it here."

The Warrior Princess was acting very stiff. He almost felt like she hated him now. Even with his lack of romantic experience,

Kuon was getting a harsh lesson in how blown timing could change things.

But he had to wring out every ounce of courage he had. Fighting the Jave wasn't nearly as scary as this.

"Th-there's something I forgot to tell you. Will you hear me out?"

"Don't worry about not being able to join the Operation. None of us blame you for that."

"Th-th-that's not it! Um, I..."

Some things were so obvious once they were pointed out, Kuon thought. Now that En had told him, it all made sense.

All this time, she'd been stuck in this weird "younger senpai" place for him, so he'd never picked up on it, but "Hanabi" was someone he couldn't let go of and wanted to protect, while "Hanabi-senpai" was someone he wanted to have pay attention to him and protect him.

On the one hand, he always wanted to be with her. On the other, he wanted her to be happy. Perhaps it was wrong to feel that way about either a young, attractive kid or an older, out-of-his-league beauty.

But maybe it didn't matter whether she was older or younger. "Senpai, I..."

He looked at Hanabi, at her tall, elegant, dramatically curved body. Her strong-willed eyes couldn't hide how anxious she felt. She had a grace to her that belied her status as the best Cavalleria the school had ever produced, but sometimes she clearly showed her age. Then he looked at her soft hands. She refused to let her talent carry her and was putting in all the work; the Fencing Kuon had taught her was slowly turning her hands into those of a swordsman.

Her long, thin fingers clutched her purse tightly. Her hands always tried so hard that Kuon couldn't help but think of them fondly. That helped him say it.

"I... I like you, senpai. I care about Suzuka Hanabi. So, make sure you come back alive."

Most likely, Hanabi's brain short-circuited.

"Y-you mean as a senpai? As a friend?"

"No..."

"Then as a Cavalleria?"

"I do like you that way, but that's not what I'm talking about."

"Th-then what...?"

Hanabi's eyes were clearly saying, *Really? Can I really believe that? Can I be happy? This is true? For real?* This expression was so unlike what she normally let herself show.

Yes, Kuon smiled. "I love you, Hanabi-senpai. As... As a woman."

"Oh... Ohhh..."

Hanabi put her hands to her face, swaying. Kuon moved to catch her. Standing so close, the difference in their height was painfully obvious. With his hand on her back to support her, he had to tilt his head all the way back, looking up at her from directly below. If he got any closer, Kuon's face would bump into her oversized boobs, so he had to be careful.

"You do...?" Hanabi said, dazed.

"Yes."

"That's...not fair. I was going to say that..."

"Sorry. You almost did, earlier...and that finally made up my mind."

"Huh? You got that?"

"En had to tell me."

"Oh, okay... That's even more unfair, Kuon-kun."

"I completely agree. Sorry," he apologized.

"You aren't sorry at all; I can tell."

"I am!"

"You have a weirdly arrogant side, you know. You're so cocky!"

"En said that, too."

"She's right."

"Sorry."

"Oh, you're apologizing when you don't mean it again."

"I do mean it," he said.

"Really?"

"Really."

"Really?" Hanabi asked once more, putting her arms around Kuon. His face naturally found its way between her massive breasts. He was wrapped in her sweet scent. "You really, really want me? I'm five years older than you. I'll be an adult way faster."

Kuon put both hands around her back. Similar questions must have been asked countless times throughout history whenever an age gap existed between two lovers, but Kuon answered in a way that only he could: "Well, I'm an old man inside."

Hanabi laughed. "I agree!"

"And if we live that long, if we live long enough for you to get old, then what could make us happier?"

"I didn't say 'old.'"

"Sorry."

"Kuon-kun," Hanabi said, touching Kuon's cheek. Her smile was happy, loving, and a little bittersweet. "I love you so, so much."

Kuon just nodded.

The bus Hanabi had taken was the last one.

Kuon and Hanabi realized there was no public transportation available to take Kuon back to the training ground. Maybe if he pushed himself, he'd be in time for the last Linear Rail, and a taxi would certainly be an option if he were willing to spring for it. Kuon had received Cavalleria pay, so money was no problem.

It was curfew and the gates were closing, so they couldn't exactly just stand around outside. Hanabi grabbed Kuon's hand and snuck him into the room she shared with Rin. It had a plush carpet and two beds with a little table between them, cute little cushions near the table, and a zabuton that was the opposite of cute. Hanabi made some tea and they drank it, talking about nothing in particular. How stressed she'd been on the date, how Rin had picked all her clothes, how surprised she'd been when he suggested they go to an onsen, how surprised he'd been when she invited him... They ate their chocolate, asking how long they'd felt this way about each other, pretty much both from the day they met, etc. Both pretended they weren't paying the clock any attention at all.

He could still go home. She could still let him.

But he didn't want to go home, and she didn't want to let him. Neither of them had ever felt like this before. They were carried away, heads in the clouds, giddily drunk on love.

Eventually, they noticed Rin hadn't come home.

Then they got a message from the headmaster saying Rin and En would be staying with her that evening. Kuon had no idea when En had disappeared; the Device itself wouldn't respond at all. It seemed to legitimately be in Sleep Mode for once.

There was a brief silence, then the same thought struck them both at once.

We're alone together until morning.

There was another brief silence, then both realized the other was thinking the same thing. They were playing a terrifying game of chicken now. It felt like whoever lost their nerve first would lose.

Kuon's mind began spinning quickly, doing the math. He felt like he'd be a failure as a man if he stood up and said it was time he got going, but also felt like if he just stayed there all night and didn't do anything, that would make him a different kind of failure. If something *did* happen, that would likely also be pretty bad. Not that he had the guts, but boy was he suddenly very conscious of how much skin Hanabi's outfit showed as she sat on her knees in that miniskirt with her hands on her thighs, fists tightly clenched, glaring at Kuon like a Bushi tensing for a fight. And so...

"It's time I got going," Kuon said. He stood up, failing as a man.

As he headed for the door, Hanabi grabbed his sleeve. He didn't need to turn around.

"Kuon-kun."

Hanabi had kept her foot on the pedal throughout the whole game of chicken, and she was the Cavalleria shipping out tomorrow.

"At ten hundred tomorrow, I'll be boarding the Mobile Mothership *Kuou*. From that point on, I'll be a Cavalleria of the Lunatic Order, serving the Imperial Air Force, Lunar Defense Force, at the back of the Capital Fall Squad. My life will belong to my companions and to all of mankind."

Kuon couldn't respond, couldn't even turn around.

Hanabi held his sleeve tight. "But until then...I'm yours."

Do what you want to do.

That got him.

Kuon turned around and took Hanabi's hand. Their fingers tightened together. Each felt how earnest those hands were, how hard they tried. Hanabi's palm was slowly growing harder, but her lips were unbelievably soft.

They sank into the night...

R IN DIDN'T COME BACK until morning.

She insisted she had no memories of where she'd been or what she'd done there, but she suddenly seemed terrified of water. *Such a shame,* Kuon thought in an extremely flat tone. *Did she have to listen to hummed radio?*

If she hadn't been in that state, she may have stopped to wonder just why Kuon was in their room that early in the morning. But she was too preoccupied to do much more than grab the luggage she'd already packed and leave with Hanabi. Kuon snuck out after them.

"Senpai, we'll have to go out together again."

"Yes, definitely," Hanabi agreed.

Kuon and Hanabi parted on the military wharf. Fuji had greeted them both already and given Kuon a nod as if acknowledging a job well done. Rin refused to even drink water.

The rest of the Fuji Squad headed toward the gate leading to the *Kuou,* leaving Kuon behind. He kept waving, trying to convince himself it would be fine, that he would see them again.

This Operation was a blitz, a huge force sent in to catch the enemy off-guard. Nearly the entire combined might of the Lunar Defense Force would drop from orbit onto the capital, smash the enemy forces, and seal the Gate. The Fuji Squad was positioned at the rear. The active Cavalleria would eliminate the main enemy forces, then the Gate Seal Squad—including the Division 5 Hanabi—would come in behind.

They'll be fine. By the time senpai drops in, most of the enemy will be gone.

If he didn't keep telling himself it would be fine, all his anxiety would come bursting out. He wanted to go with them, even if he had to do it in his temp frame.

He couldn't calm the qualms in his chest.

The final adjustments to his new frame ended without issue, five days earlier than scheduled. The development engineers had really pushed themselves.

It felt like summer vacation had begun at school. Kuon spent every day going between school and the training grounds, but it had been weeks since he attended any classes. He'd been going through the front gates and right to the garage without ever stopping by class 1-A, so he'd completely forgotten about vacation.

There were still plenty of students there doing self-training. Kuon wandered through them, heading for the training ground at the garage. The oversized DM rocket booster pointing to the heavens was his guide. *Like the smokestack on a sento,* the bath-addicted ex-Hero thought.

Cicadas sang in his ears and the humid summer wind brushed his face as Kuon faced his new partner. It was a brand-new blue frame, standing on unmowed grass.

En gazed up at it like it was blinding.

"They call it the Soukyu (Pleiades)," she told Kuon. "The base is the Division 1 Soukyu. They added additional disposable boosters all around it and strengthened the close-range combat capabilities to enhance Machine Fencing. It also inherited the special weapon that Master uses, along with the Pleiades subtitle."

"Amazing..."

"Isn't it?" En said proudly, although she'd had nothing to do with making it.

Kuon stared up at the slim silhouette of the DM in awe. It shone in the light like a blue-armored warrior.

The mass-produced model had been shaved, tucked, tightened, and honed. The Pleiades had been fitted to its left shoulder, and the frame sported a long, rectangular backpack like a collapsed fan on its back with a ridiculous number of boosters.

Ah. Saying they'd strengthened close-quarters capabilities was a positive spin on what they'd actually done, which was lighten the frame by removing all the sensors and stabilizers that assisted with ranged-combat. This thing likely didn't even have a lock-on, yet its back and shoulders had boosters larger than the frame itself. Kuon thought it looked like it was shouldering a bunch of birdcages.

"Mm, those boosters make it look all slapped together. They're totally in the way," he commented.

"What are you talking about, Kuon-sama?! Those were specifically added to compensate for your lack of magic!"

"Oh, right." That made sense. He chose to be grateful for them. The head developer gave him a detailed rundown as well as the new Device. The frame returned to the Device, and Kuon went back to the training grounds.

Two days passed since Hanabi had left, and he was scheduled for three more days of hard training, though that could go longer depending on how fast he learned.

What was going on with the Operation? He'd heard nothing more. Was the Fuji Squad still on standby aboard the *Kuou*? Or was the Operation already over, and everyone was getting ready to come home?

He wanted to see Hanabi again.

For the first time, Suzuka Hachishiki's soul learned how painful it was to be separated from the one you love.

"How many years have I been teaching you?" Kaede asked.

Why was she staring into the distance like that? Kuon wondered. A gust of wind blew across the training ground.

"Twelve years in my last life, seven in this one, so nineteen years total."

"Hmm," his master muttered. "Surprisingly short."

"Is it?"

"Not many Cavalleria could get this good at Shichisei Kenbu in only nineteen years. I suppose even an idiot can get somewhere if he tries hard."

Kuon found her behavior unsettling. Nothing good ever happened when Kaede gave out compliments.

"Let me ask you something. Don't answer me as Suzuka Hachishiki, but as Okegawa Kuon."

"Okay."

"Answer directly from the heart—are you ready to throw your life away?"

Okegawa Kuon answered immediately. "I am."

He failed to notice the shadow that crossed her face.

This extremely simple question was asked of anyone inheriting Shichisei Kenbu. Seven generations ago, it had taken the student two months to arrive at the answer, and four generations ago, the student had taken six months. The last student—Kaede herself—had answered correctly the first time. Not because she was highly skilled, Kaede knew, but because it was simply a matter of personality. Many would consider it a trick question.

Suzuka Hachishiki and Okegawa Kuon had both done well. She had never thought it would be time to ask this question after only nineteen years. He may have no talent for magic, but he did for Fencing. She felt a light from this student that made her think he did, at least. But even so, or perhaps doubly so, Kaede's mind was made up.

"Shame," she said. "You can't learn the ultimate art."

Kuon's mind nearly went blank with confusion. He couldn't understand it. He'd been thrown in a river and nearly died, brought to low-oxygen environments and nearly died, seen his friends head off to war with his heart breaking, and trained as if his life depended on it. After all that, this? Why?

"Can I ask," he said, barely able to contain his rage, "the reason?"

"Sorry. Rules say I can't tell you."

"Master!"

"I said sorry. I'm apologizing. Is that not satisfactory?"

"We've only got seven years until the Queen returns! I can't afford to get stuck here!"

"That's the problem. You're still trying to do it all on your—no, never mind."

"Master!" he protested, but Kaede cut him off.

"Don't."

He could hear his teeth grinding. He'd put up with so much unfair crap from her, but this was beyond reason.

"Master!" En yelled, appearing out of nowhere in a panic.

Kuon was about to yell, "Not now!" but...

"The Operation...the Squads!" En stammered. Both Kuon and Kaede realized the Guide was upset for an entirely different reason.

"What?" Kaede demanded. En looked at Kuon. "Go ahead and say it," Kaede urged.

En broke the bad news.

"The Imperial Air Force, Lunar Defense Force, Capital Fall Squad main force...has been massacred..."

This time, Kuon's mind really did go blank.

"Remember what I said to you before you began training!" Kaede said. "Are you going to make the same mistake again? Christ, get your head straight already, you idiot!"

After hearing En's report, Kuon had run out of the training grounds, Kaede's words falling on deaf ears. He didn't want to hear them. If she kicked him out again, he would never be allowed back this time around, but who cared about that?

Kuon ran all the way to the school. A state of emergency had been declared, so all public transportation was down. The shopping district was a ghost town. He raced through streets he'd walked through with Hanabi just two days ago, headed toward the garage's training ground at top speed.

The main force had been massacred.

In the Air Force, "massacred" didn't mean *everyone* was dead; rather, the term was used when at least 60 percent of the frontline Cavalleria had been rendered incapable of combat. The remaining 40 percent might be rescuing injured compatriots, beginning the retreat, or otherwise unable to complete their operational goals.

Was the Fuji Squad part of that 60 percent?

Unlikely. They had been at the rear of the main force, and Hanabi said the plan was for them to drop down after the main force had cleared the enemies around the Gate.

But if that had changed? If the Fuji Squad had been added to the main force?

It probably hadn't. *They* probably hadn't. But he couldn't say that for sure. He couldn't predict every action Command would take. Perhaps Fuji, Rin, and Hanabi were out there right now, trying to escape the Jave, trying to save injured Cavalleria in other squads, perhaps grievously injured themselves, or even worse. The Jave might have...attacked, eaten...Hanabi, the girl from that day, the same fate...

Run! Run, run run run run run!

"Kuon-sama!" En shrieked. "What are you doing?!"

"Isn't it obvious?! I'm going to fly out of the training ground and land in the capital!"

The black mist covering the capital repelled all invaders. It didn't allow light or electric waves, and it disrupted magic. It even stripped the DM right off you. It was a powerful barrier.

But the higher up you went, the thinner it got. That's why the Imperial Air Force had fired cannons down on the capital from orbit, scattering the mist, then dropped troops in...

"Are you a complete idiot? Think for a second! You'll never get high enough without a shuttle!"

"Sure I can. I've got the extra boosters, a shield, the Witch Bubble and...and with *that*, a sixth generation DM can do it."

His eyes locked on the academy training grounds, on its landmark, the object thrusting toward the sky.

The DM Rocket Booster.

"I'll follow the same trajectory as the Mobile Mothership *Kuou*. Up to orbit above, then drop directly down."

"Hnnngggh..."

"I did atmospheric descents several times in my previous life. No point in trying to stop me, I'm going."

"Hnnngggggghh..."

"You don't have to come."

But the Guide shook her head. "No. No, Kuon-sama, I will be joining you."

"Don't blame me if Master chews you out."

"I'm still moving, aren't I? She hasn't cut the magic link. That's her answer: 'Watch over my idiot student so he doesn't die.' That's my purpose."

"Sounds rough."

"But Kuon-sama...try not to make her sad."

He reached the training ground. The storage shed with the rocket was locked up, his entrance prevented by a heavy door and electronic lock with over 300,000,000 possible passwords.

"En..."

"Okay, okay." The little fairy inserted a digital key into the control panel. There was a click and the door opened easily. "What was your backup plan if I wasn't here?"

"Smash the door in."

How violent, thought En.

The two of them raced down the dark hallway. After opening a third door, Kuon was able to minimally deploy his DM, and, after the fifth, in a dark, silent, windless hangar, he finally responded to En's request.

"I don't want to make her sad," he said, his voice echoing.

"It sure doesn't seem like it."

"Master isn't part of the operation because of the time limit?"

"That, plus a fair amount of spite directed at the military, yes."

When Kuon was ten years old in this life, Nanahoshi Kaede, still officially part of the military, had been deployed with the Lunar Defense Force to fight Jave invading Jogen waters. The actions of humanity's strongest Cavalleria saved Jogen that day, but the wounds she received in that battle had ended her military career. The magic release required to deploy a DM meant she could only keep one active for five minutes. The real reason she'd been so scornful in her mock battle against the Fuji Squad was because Fuji hadn't attempted to force a long-term fight.

As Kuon and his Guide bypassed the final lock, they found themselves facing the giant rocket booster. Connecting his DM to it, Kuon asked En to crunch the numbers to find the best point of re-entry over the capital.

"If you can open comms to the squad, please do. I want all the intel I can get."

"Sheesh, you sure work a Device hard." Even as she joked, a vast number of windows popped up on his field of vision, channeled through the magic link to his DM. En quickly organized them, doing her best to let Kuon know the current status of the Imperial Air Force, Lunar Defense Force, and Capital Fall Squad.

Then she whispered, "Booster, fire."

A satellite in orbit picked up the signal from the surface. Far to the southeast of the imperial mainland, in the school grounds on the eastern part of Jogen Island in the Pacific, a Division 1 bristling with additional boosters and thermal armor flashed a single light and launched an instant later.

With G-forces threatening to crush his organs, Kuon tried assessing the situation. The Fall Squad was beginning to retreat. The main force had been massacred, and the remaining 40 percent were scattered and fleeing, trying to get outside the range of the Jave. Mobile Mothership *Kuou* was on standby in orbit, as were the rear squads. So the Fuji Squad and the Lunatic Order...

He swore under his breath.

His squad had been dropped on the capital just before the order to retreat. Kuon's Soukyu (Pleiades) became a shooting star, hurtling across the sky toward them. It was less a rocket launch than an intercontinental missile. He passed through the clouds and the sky gradually turned from blue to black. The main booster's fuel ran out, and it broke away...

"Kuon-sama, bad news," En said. As she spoke, his radar showed a swarm of manta-like flying Jave coming toward them, blocking their path. If he tried going around them, it could delay him for hours.

He never hesitated.

"Punching through."

En sighed with what Kuon knew was half "sheesh" and half "attaboy."

_//////////⌐

It had been a long time since she'd descended to the capital.

As they entered the atmosphere, Hanabi was feeling pretty good. She could look directly at the black moon now without a panic attack. All it reminded her of was the lecture the kid had given her in the water, of his kindness, warmth, and familiar scent.

The main force had been dropped five minutes earlier. A barrage of missiles scattered the mist over the capital, and their senpai dropped through the hole. The Fuji Squad would follow soon after, leading the Lunatic Order. They placed descent boards under their feet, handling the wall of fire generated on re-entry via adiabatic compression.

The DM's full powers would activate after re-entry. As they reached the air just above the capital, the main squad would wipe out the Jave in aerial combat and seal the Gate.

Their comms were still active. Hanabi spoke briefly to Fuji and Rin, waiting for their moment to act.

Re-entry in five, four, three, two…

There was a roar and a powerful jolt from below. The descent boards and Witch Bubbles couldn't lessen the G-forces entirely, so Hanabi, the Fuji Squad, and the other two advance Lunatic Order Squads had to endure them as they all entered the gravitational field.

The light around her reflected, all red and orange and multi-colored, and her eyes both saw and didn't see it as she desperately waited for it to end. Comms were cut off for the entirety of the two-minute descent. Enduring pressure that seemed ready to crush her, Kuon's face floated into Hanabi's mind.

I'll come back to you.

At last they were through the wall of fire, but they were still falling at terrifying speeds. They continued decelerating.

It had been thirteen years since she'd seen the capital.

Hanabi was back in the skies above her home.

It was hell.

The spectacle below her wasn't the home she'd known. Red fleshy monsters—the manta-shaped flying Jave—were assaulting the main force. Hanabi's senpai was devoured before they even had a chance to take up positions. The comms came back online but were filled with screams. Command was issuing orders right and left, the result a confused mess. The numbers Hanabi saw below her and the numbers on her radar were automatically added together.

The total was nearly three times the combined might of the Lunar Defense Force.

As Hanabi stared, stunned, something red flew past her at high speed; a flying manta. The Cavalleria next to Hanabi was gone. She'd been an attacker from the current rank three team, a friend Hanabi had fought many a mock battle against. Her friend's arm fell from the manta's mouth. Hanabi realized her friend had been eaten by a Jave, and only then did she register the alarms blaring in her ears.

They were surrounded by dozens of Jave. They circled the freshly descended Student Echelons like sharks circling their prey, then suddenly wheeled around to attack.

What...the...

In the two minutes comms had been down, the Jave had attacked. Hanabi knew that much.

"Watch your six! Form up around me! Leave no blind spots! They're coming!"

Fuji's orders snapped her out of it. "Form two rings around Controls! Attackers in the outer ring, Gunners in the inner! Do it now if you don't want to die!"

The Lunatic Order Cavalleria had frozen, making themselves

prime targets, but now they all snapped into action. Three Squads, three Controls, three Cavalleria back to back, three Gunners just in front of them, and five Attackers protecting the gaps. Hanabi's friend, the sixth Attacker, was already gone.

"Lunatic Order Sagara Squad, Mitsuhashi Squad, any objections to me assuming command? Then both Controls, fire with the Gunners! Send all intel you receive my way! Attackers, they're on us!"

Their orders had changed.

The three Lunatic Order squads led by Fuji were to rendezvous with the third wave of drop squads and assist with the retreat of what remained of the main force. Retreat was the only goal. Command had given up on attacking the Gate. *A wise decision,* Fuji felt. All that remained was to extract as many senpai from the center of the enemy as possible. If they could get out of the capital war zone through Tokyo Bay and reach the escape fleet on the Pacific, they might be safe. The black mist might prevent entry, but it didn't block escape. You couldn't even see the mist from the inside. The only barrier to escaping was the Jave themselves.

They'd gone up against ten-to-one odds before. They'd faced ten times their number and killed their enemies instantly, sustaining no damage. Now they were up against only three times their number, with eleven Cavalleria. They may have been students, but they were highly skilled.

But none of this was nearly good enough.

It was all the Lunatic Order could do to protect themselves

until reinforcements dropped down from above, much less go to help the main forces.

If Kuon were here...

Fuji knew he could stop time, calculate enemy attacks and evasion routes, and share them with the rest of the squad by using Shichisei Kenbu: Mod. Tensetsu Shigure.

If only Okegawa Kuon were here, they wouldn't be struggling against these enemies.

Why had the operation been for now? Why not a week later, even five days later? If it had, Okegawa Kuon would have been there with them. They never would have been forced to watch a friend die.

He knew it was too late and was surprised to find himself dwelling on it anyway.

Since when am I so reliant on him? On a thirteen-year-old Division 1 child?

Pathetic, he thought. *No point wishing for what you don't have. Focus on how to get out of this with what you do.*

The third wave of reinforcements was coming; they would be defenseless. The Lunatic Order needed to clear the trash out of the sky for them. Keeping their formation, they began to rise.

It was Rin's first time descending on the capital.

Unlike Hanabi, Rin was born and raised on Jogen, and had never set foot on the mainland. She'd never even done a re-entry before. Before she could catch her breath, they were in the thick of it. Rin hadn't even gotten her bearings yet when she found herself sniping the attacking monsters. She was in a panic, her mind totally blank. She couldn't think. Her body just did what Fuji said, moving where he told her, returning fire.

I'm getting tired fast...

She didn't realize that until their reinforcements had arrived and they were headed to the Gate to support the main force's retreat. Her magic was draining at nearly twice the speed it usually did. Hanabi was at the fore, shielding the others, and had opened a comm to ask if Rin was okay. *How perceptive,* Rin thought. "I'm a goner! Hanabi, protect me!"

"Sure, got it," Hanabi said in a manly voice, as if sensing just how far gone Rin was. *You don't have to be Kyuu-kun to fall for that.* Laughing to herself, Rin followed. She had three magic recovery capsules left. If those ran out, she wouldn't be able to keep her DM up, and she'd be eaten by those gross, squiggly monsters.

Rin would rather have Hanabi kill her than let that happen. The Warrior Princess could play the role of seppuku assistant. This was a silly thought, and even as she thought it, another part of her mind was thinking about the boy who'd stolen her friend's heart. If he'd been here, this would be so much easier.

The Lunatic Order hurried toward the Gate, where their compatriots were trapped with no escape route.

The survivors of the main force began withdrawing, thanks to the efforts of the Fuji Squad and their reinforcements, but those were only the survivors furthest from the Gate. In the war zone near the Gate, there were still several squads putting up a desperate resistance against the Jave. The Fuji Squad wanted to go save the rest, but it was all they could do just to save those close at hand. If they took any risks, they'd end up waiting for salvation themselves.

An hour after the operation had begun, the battlefield remained under the Jave's control. The Fuji Squad was surrounded by enemies on all sides, struggling to save as many Cavalleria as they could. "We're out of time," Fuji said. "If we stay any longer, the ships that are here for us will leave. Let's go."

No one argued; they all thought it was a wise decision. All members of the three squads temporarily under Fuji's control assented, except for one.

"You go on ahead," Suzuka Hanabi said. "I'm gonna cut my way closer to the Gate."

There was a stunned silence. Did she want to die here?

"You can't!" Rin screamed like the demons had a hold of her.

But Hanabi just shook her head. "Sorry. I have to do this. Let me go."

"I said you can't! Are you trying to get yourself killed? Make yourself into a hero that way?!"

"No, Rin. I'm not."

"Kyuu-kun said you admire the Hero so much he's afraid you've got a death wish! This is exactly what he meant!" Rin cried. "What's wrong with you?! I thought you'd learned better than to just charge in!"

"If the Hero hadn't saved me, I wouldn't even be here."

"So what?!"

"I was right under the Gate. That area was abandoned. There was no one coming to save me, but *he* came. He didn't abandon me." Hanabi smiled. "I can still fight. I'm Division 5. I'm a Maneuver Cavalleria. I don't want to abandon anyone like me."

They'd known each other long enough for Rin to realize there was nothing she could say to change Hanabi's mind, but she tried anyway. She had to. "Don't you want to see Kyuu-kun again?!" she pleaded, tears running down her face.

"I..." Hanabi didn't have an answer for that one. If she said anything, it would weaken her resolve.

"Then I'm coming with you! If you try and stop me, I'll just follow you anyway!" Rin said, wiping her tears. "If you don't want that, then don't go!"

"Rin...really...?" Hanabi looked at Fuji for help.

But Fuji had no intention of helping. "Sorry, everyone," he said. "I'm disbanding the provisional squad. Sagara Squad, Mitsuhashi Squad, head for the ship."

"Fuji-kun, you can't mean—"

"I'm coming with you, Suzuka-kun," Fuji snorted. "If you don't want that, then don't go."

"Argh!" Hanabi let out, clutching her head. She was at a total loss. "You're both idiots."

"Says who?!" both Squad Leader and Subleader said as one.

So many times he'd thought he was done for.

The Cavalleria had descended as part of the main Lunar Defense Force, part of a squad ordered to destroy the four flesh pillars placed near the Gate. There weren't that many Jave around that area just then. Immediately after dropping in, they'd pro-ceeded as planned, easily eliminating the flesh pillars believed to control the Gate. That much was successful.

But a moment later, the Gate opened and an insane number of Jave came flying out. The timing was so precise that an awful thought struck the Cavalleria.

That wasn't a control device...it was a switch.

A switch which triggered if anyone tried harming the Gate. Instead of an alarm, it summoned dark red fleshy monsters. In the blink of an eye, his fellow squad members were nearly all shot, eaten, or otherwise dead, and only then did the Cavalleria make his frozen body flee for his life. He didn't know which way he was going; he just flew away until his magic ran out and he crashed. The road he landed on was so covered in blood and flesh you couldn't even see the asphalt under it, the gore so mangled he couldn't tell if it was human or Jave.

He looked up to find three mantas headed straight for him. They couldn't even be bothered to fire light bullets. They must be real gourmets. Better to eat a human alive then use a projectile to kill them first.

This is it.

He had enough magic for a single rifle shot. He stuck it in his own mouth. Dying was better than getting eaten alive. Before he could fire, a wave of light enveloped the mantas, exterminating them.

"Are you okay?"

A goddess spoke to him, a beauty the likes of which he'd never seen landing right before him. Her DM sported massive wings and a gigantic rifle, far beyond what a Division 3 like him could ever wield.

"You're the last one," the goddess said, shaking her ponytail. "If you can still move, you should run. I'll buy you time."

Another DM landed beside her. A boy with the look of an officer tossed him a capsule. "Orders are to retreat," said the boy. "Fly north, then turn east at Kanda. If you head straight out to sea you should find the escape fleet."

"Wh-what will you do…?"

"Hold the enemy off. If we go with you, they'll follow after."

"Oh…thanks…"

He swallowed the capsule and began flying north, as he was told. There were so few enemies. They must have cut a path for him. Only then did he realize who those Cavalleria were.

The Lunatic Order. Students.

They should have been on standby at the rear, yet here they were on the front lines, covering his retreat. They even gave him their precious recovery capsules.

Please don't die.

All he could do was pray for them. The last survivor of the main force flew off toward the escape fleet so the students' mission could succeed.

"Whew," Rin said. She landed listlessly on the ground, clearly thoroughly exhausted. She was completely out of magic recovery capsules. She'd used all of hers ages back, and Fuji had given his last to that Cavalleria. Fuji was on the ground next to her, catching his breath. Maintaining flight had become actively painful.

There were no enemies nearby, but Rin, Fuji, and Hanabi all knew better. They were surrounded, with nowhere to run. The enemy might not be in view, but their radar told a different story. It showed a ring of Jave surrounding them.

They were moving in. The circle was getting smaller.

So this is finally it. No sooner had this thought crossed Rin's mind than a transmission came in from over ten thousand kilometers above. It was from the Fuji Squad's newest member, who'd ditched his ultimate arts training, punched through the Jave swarm, and was about to begin the re-entry process.

"Senpai! Hanabi-senpai!"

Hanabi was out front, preparing to fire at the enemy. Her back twitched. Rin and Fuji's reactions were more or less the same.

"Kuon-kun...?" Hanabi looked up, as if she couldn't believe it.

You idiot, Rin thought. *Don't sound so happy.*

"What's going on down there? The main force has retreated, right? Why are you still in enemy territory?"

Each of them responded in their own way. "They retreated because we fought to let them get away! You should be thanking us," Hanabi snapped.

"Kyuu-kun, feel free to call her an idiot for us, and to call us idiots for staying here with her," Rin said.

"I appreciate you coming," Fuji responded. "I'm sending you our coordinates. But don't think you have to make the drop. I leave the judgment call to you."

Their focus was beginning to fray and their bodies felt heavy, exhaustion making their vision blurry. Hanabi was Division 5 and could still fight, but Fuji and Rin were almost out of magic.

The voice from above gave the squad hope. "Roger that. I'm fully aware of both your courage and what colossal idiots you all can be."

"Ahahaha, you're calling us idiots? You sound like the headmaster."

"I'm coming to save you. I would never abandon you. So please, don't die before I get there."

Rin made an impressed noise, Fuji nodded as if to say he was waiting, and Hanabi turned to face her companions, looking extremely proud.

"See? My Kuon-kun is the best. The greatest!"

Rin waved a hand, conceding defeat. "Okay, you win, he is. Your precious Kyuu-kun."

"I completely underestimated the boy," Fuji said. "You were right about him, Suzuka-kun."

Even if he was too late...

Even if they all died here...

How much time would it take him to cross the wall of flames and get to them? The boy couldn't even fly. Could they survive that long? The answer was obvious, but it didn't matter. For a cocky, arrogant old man in a boy's body, that Division 1 kid had a strange strength. He'd come running, having never given up on them, and that was all that mattered.

But only Rin and Fuji thought that way. "Kuon-kun," Hanabi

said, as if there was nothing in this world that could scare her now. "We'll be here waiting."

"Got it, Hanabi-senpai."

There was a crackle, and the transmission cut out. It didn't matter to Hanabi if that was caused by combat or re-entry. Either way, she knew he was coming.

She stopped looking up and focused her eyes in front of her. The sky was blotted out by Jave, all after the three of them. The swarm was thickest in front of them, and the Gate loomed behind those monsters.

Hanabi popped her last capsule into her mouth. Her field of vision narrowed, turning red, and her heart raced. The capsules were definitely not good for you, but they could restore your magic in an instant. It felt like her blood was flowing backward, but she forced that sensation back and grinned. She wasn't scared of anything. Kuon-kun was coming.

Hanabi launched herself forward, drawing the enemy toward her to protect the two behind her.

The fires of Suzuka Hanabi's life were raging, bursting like the fireworks she was named after. She fired her massive Scout Nova Rifle at the swarm in front of her. The explosion was like a sun appearing on the surface of the Earth. The clouds being blown away showed the path of the shockwave. Any Jave caught up in the explosion were vaporized instantly.

After her magic light beam destroyed the first wave of enemies, she turned her rifle, sweeping away all the Jave around them. A fifth of the enemy on the radar were now gone. She fired a second and third time. Even monsters could learn a little; the manta fired bullets of their own, all targeting Hanabi's rifle shots and shooting them down. "Clever," she muttered. She deployed her Servants, liquifying any enemy that got within range.

She was only able to keep this fight going for less than ten minutes.

On the other hand, lasting nearly ten minutes against over-whelming odds was quite impressive. After getting the transmission from Okegawa Kuon, the Fuji Squad held back the Jave swarm with everything they had left.

At the front, Hanabi used the full force of her Type-3 Artillery to blow away the enemy. Just behind her, Rin's support fire took care of any mantas that got in Hanabi's blind spots. Back-to-back with Rin, Fuji's Control monitored the flow of combat and made sure Hanabi knew what actions to take next.

This was what they'd considered their optimal arrangement before Okegawa Kuon joined the squad. They'd had a senpai Attacker the year before, but after that person graduated the team had only grown stronger, and they'd been convinced adding one or even two new members would likely not improve their effectiveness as a team. While it would increase their options, they ultimately believed a new member would be detrimental to their overall prowess.

And they'd been right. At least until Okegawa Kuon learned to fight as part of a team.

The Shichisei Kenbu that Kuon brought not only expanded their options, it had dramatically improved them. Their win rate had gone from a highly-ranked "stable" to "unbeatable."

But Okegawa Kuon wasn't there yet. This was previously their best formation, but Fuji and Rin were already at their limit.

When Hanabi's remaining magic crossed the 30 percent threshold, support fire and Control went silent. The squad members at Hanabi's rear were no longer able to maintain their DMs. All they could do was stay out of Hanabi's way, maintaining silence to avoid distracting her, waiting for the inevitable.

The Jave swarm filled Hanabi's vision. She couldn't let her concentration drop for an instant.

The manta swarm fired at her. Enemies that only appeared as red blips on her radar exploded in balls of fire, but, by the time they did, they'd already fired invisible bullets her way. Her DM sounded the alarm. One hundred and thirty-two shots were headed right for her.

Kuon-kun is coming, she whispered to herself. Saying it out loud gave her strength. Her evasive maneuvers couldn't avoid all the shots, and several of them burst upon her Witch Bubble. Several others made it through the barrier and blew bits of her armor off, but these attacks were normally powerful enough to kill a human instantly, so getting off this lightly was a godsend. The radar on her left shoulder went down, and the fragments scratched her forehead, drawing blood. The DM's Witch Bubble had a simple healing function and soon sealed the wound, trying to restore her to combat readiness.

But the blood covering half her head had rattled Hanabi. *This isn't right,* she thought. This wasn't how she fought nowadays.

This was how she fought when she was alone. But she had companions now.

Hanabi spun around. A ground Jave was reaching its tentacles out toward Rin, ready to eat her.

A disgusting, quivering mass was approaching. Writhing tentacles were flailing everywhere, slowly, as if it wanted her to panic.

Just kill me quickly, Rin thought.

Jave preferred to consume humans alive. They loved toying with their food, which wasn't as much fun for the one being eaten. That last Cavalleria they'd saved had been just about to kill himself. Come to think of it, she'd been planning to ask Hanabi to do the honors. She looked at Hanabi, who was slicing away the Jave while running toward them with a horrible expression.

But it was too late. The monster was moving faster now, trying to eat her before Hanabi got there. *At least this way it won't toy with me,* Rin thought. Or maybe Hanabi would go for the mercy kill.

Sorry. And thank you, Hanabi.

Stay close to Kyuu-kun.

Rin closed her eyes and waited, but the moment never came. *Huh?* she thought as she opened her eyes.

A goddess stood before Rin. A goddess with a hole in her guts, spilling blood on the tentacle growing out of her stomach.

Hanabi had blocked the blow meant to kill Rin with her own body. As Rin howled, Hanabi's blood spattered on Rin's cheeks. Drops of that blood mingled with tears as they rolled off Rin's face.

Hanabi turned, slashing once with her Blade. It cut away the Jave's tentacle that had pierced her. The Witch Bubble tried sealing the wound, and, as it did, Rin spoke, her voice shaking. "What are you *doing*, Hanabi?!"

"Why are you giving up, Rin?"

"You... You could survive on your own if you had to! What are you thinking?"

"I'm going to save you," Hanabi said, coughing up blood. "I'm not abandoning anyone, even if you tell me to. If you don't want that, then don't die!"

"You're an idiot..."

"You're one to talk."

Hanabi deployed six Servant Blades. She shielded the immobilized pair behind her, raising her own Blades high as if promising she wouldn't let a single Jave pass. No more flying or ranged attacks, just close quarters combat on the ground, all Fencing. Her master was the rightful heir to Shichisei Kenbu, Okegawa Kuon.

He will come.

Her Blades were backed up by magic and faith. They would protect her precious friends.

Fuji had a frame optimized for Control. Forcing his fraying mind into action, he managed to activate a small portion of his DM. The one part he'd manifested was a highly-sensitive receptor with more processing power than a high-end AI Device. He channeled the information on enemy positions, pathed them out, and linked those predictions to Hanabi.

This gave Suzuka Hanabi artificially enhanced 360-degree vision. Theoretically, it removed all her blind spots, enhanced her fencer's eye—giving her swords a veritable bird's-eye view—and completed her protective barrier. This went far beyond having eyes in the back of her head: Hanabi could see everything. If something tried attacking Fuji behind her, she could block it with her Servant Blades.

Hanabi and her six Servant Blades formed a circle around the tapped-out, wounded, immobile pair. The Jave had no concept of fear, but the sight of seven gleaming Blades stopped their assault.

The Cavalleria who'd been saved by the Hero, admired the Hero, and was now becoming a hero in her own right, said softly, "Come at me."

It was like there were seven of Hanabi.

The Servant Blades moved like they were held by invisible fencers, cutting down any and all Jave that came after Fuji and Rin. Never the brightest of creatures, the Jave went after not the Blades, but their unseen wielders. These attacks only met empty air and led to the Jave's defeats.

Hanabi's consciousness was split in seven, operating both the Blade in her hands and the six Servant Blades simultaneously. This took astonishing amounts of magic and concentration and wasn't sustainable for very long. Still coughing up blood, covered in the blood of the slain, buffeted by the ceaseless attacks, sustaining wound after wound, Hanabi still refused to falter.

Suzuka Hanabi—the Hero—stood her ground.

In Rin's eyes, it looked like Hanabi was converting the light of her very life energy into strength and fighting with it. The longer she drew this out, the longer she protected them, the closer Suzuka Hanabi's death came. Yet Rin knew Hanabi would never turn and run. She would never abandon them.

Slice, thrust, cut, swing forward, backslash, strong hit, parry and strike, trip, quick draw, stab, side strike, rain slash, right, left, overhead blow, reverse...

Each blow was precise, every cut good enough to end this. The Fencing that Okegawa Kuon had taught Hanabi was saving their lives even as it drained away her own.

Rin screamed like she'd gone mad. "Kyuu-kun! Kyuu-kun, Kyuu-kun! Kyuu-kun!" With no magic of her own left, Rin watched helplessly as the light of Hanabi's life force threatened to burst like a firework against the night sky. Unable to tear her eyes away, she continued shrieking. "Kyuu-kun! Hurry, please! Hanabi... Hanabi's going to die! Kyuu-kun!"

Next to her, Fuji was clutching his side, staring up at the blue sky above. His bleeding refused to stop. "Okegawa-kun..." he whispered. "How much longer...?"

Then, the skies above changed—

For the worse.

As the number of Jave slowly whittled away, the Gate behind them opened.

Schaaaaaaa...

The Jave scattered like newborn spiders, completely clearing the path between them and the dimensional passage. It was as if the monsters were rolling out the red carpet.

A horrible chill ran through Hanabi. Her instincts screamed at her to withdraw. She had to mobilize every ounce of courage she had left just to stay put.

The Gate was 300 meters across. A massive Jave appeared from beyond the dimensional barrier, one almost as large as the Gate itself. It was disk-shaped, like the surface Jave, but, instead of dark purple, it was a shade of red that reminded Hanabi of internal organs. She'd never seen this type before; it was a total unknown with mouths all over it. The mouths yawned open, spewing countless flying Jave.

Staring at it, stunned, Hanabi realized this was the Queen.

She didn't know this same Queen had fought Suzuka Hachishiki, and that he'd been unable to finish her off for good.

Have you ever been surrounded by dozens of enemies? Have you ever been stared down by hundreds out for your blood? Can you even imagine how horrifying that is if they aren't even human?

But Kuon-kun is coming.

By nature, Hanabi was more easily frightened than most, and she had maintained her sanity while surrounded by countless monsters by chanting those words like a spell.

But her chant faded away in the face of this Queen and the flood of monsters she spewed.

"Ah..."

Kuon wasn't coming. She'd tried waiting for him, but he still wasn't here.

He wasn't going to make it.

Light faded from the barrier of Blades, and the Servants fell to the ground. Hanabi's knees crumpled. Her heart had folded. "Kuon-kun..." she whispered.

Skreeeeeeeeeeeeeeeeeeeeeeeeeeeeeeeeeeeeeeeee!

An insane shriek came from the Jave around her, so loud she forgot to cover her ears. The air shook so fast that all other sound died away. Her body was wracked by it, shaken to the core. Hanabi's mind and heart were paralyzed with fear, leaving her unable to move a finger. She could feel a warm liquid leaking out from her nether regions. She felt no shame.

That shriek was the Jave victory cry.

I'm going to die, Hanabi thought.

The monsters' celebration began.

This was revenge for all the Jave Hanabi had slaughtered, joy over obtaining the best meal—a Division 5—and frenzy at the sight of their Queen for the first time in over a decade.

The Jave loved to eat humans alive, Rin had explained. This was true. They loved fresh magic. Magic was the energy of life, and only faint traces of it could be harvested from corpses. That was why the Jave swallowed humans whole whenever possible, slowly digesting them inside their bodies. Since their entire species did as such, the Jave wouldn't drive humanity to extinction. They were taking care to let a few humans live, not eating too many. Getting too greedy and leaving nothing left to eat was why they'd been forced to burn so much magic opening a Gate to this world.

Even monsters could learn.

In the world beyond the Gate, there had been humans with a special talent, able to use magic without wearing a DM. They were called witches. Humans had used witches' powers in war, transforming them into Jave. For the first three years, they'd maintained control over that power, but, out of anger, despair, and hunger, the monsters that were once witches turned on mankind. They attacked, killed, and devoured. Memories of when they'd been witches vanished, their very souls becoming monstrous. Humanity had vanished from the world. Then, they opened a Gate.

It would be some time in the future before the humans of this world would learn that.

As Hanabi sat, dazed, the Jave Queen drew closer. She seemed to be moving much slower than she actually was. She was just so big that she gave the illusion of sluggishness. As she descended toward Hanabi, she stretched out hundreds of long tentacles.

Hanabi was confused to find herself somehow still sane. Behind her, she heard Rin screaming. *Stand up! Run! What are you doing?!* Hearing this without actually listening, Hanabi understood the reason she'd survived as a child. Potential magic didn't change, no matter how old you were; it was set at birth. Since Hanabi had always been a Division 5, the Jave that day were saving her for their Queen. That's why they hadn't killed her, hadn't eaten her, and tried capturing her alive, she realized.

She was right.

The Gate was maintained by Jave magic. To maintain the sheer size of it, the Queen entered their world once every decade or so, her appearances matching the rate at which Division 5s appeared. The last Cavalleria the Fuji Squad rescued had been half right: The four flesh pillars *were* switches, but they weren't automatic. The Jave Queen lurked inside the Gate, keeping it open, and she could detect when someone strong enough to destroy her kind had appeared.

The injuries another human had given the Queen thirteen years ago were not yet healed, but she wasn't about to let this meal go uneaten. What had brought the Queen here was unmistakably Hanabi's magic.

If Suzuka Hanabi had been snatched up here, she would have spent at least seven days being tortured inside the Jave's body, her magic slowly drained away. Nerve-corrupting tentacles would have inserted themselves into her mind through her mouth, nose, and ears, scooping out Hanabi's memories, slurping up what made her *her*, and destroying her very mind.

If she had been snatched up here.

But it had been more than ten minutes since they got word that a DM belonging to no other squad was going to drop from orbit from the Mobile Mothership *Kuou*. A full minute had passed since the Cavalleria who'd destroyed the flesh pillars spotted a comet over the Pacific.

The Jave around them were in a frenzy, ready to see their Queen have her way with Hanabi. The Queen, having been forced to flee without eating the previous ultimate snack—Suzuka Hachishiki—was too hungry to notice.

Hanabi herself was petrified, too afraid of the horrifying number of tentacles streaking toward her. The world in front of her no longer seemed real. It was like she was gazing at a distant memory, at the tentacles that had reached out for her in that burning town years ago. She could no longer remember who it was she loved.

And yet...

Shichisei Kenbu.

Hanabi heard those words. She thought she was hallucinating. She was all alone in a burning town, the Jave Queen's tentacles about to grab her, and Kuon wasn't coming.

Hanabi thought she was about to be tortured to death.

As she stood, surrounded by Jave, she saw her younger self surrounded by flames. Little Hanabi turned and spoke to her: "But I know he's coming," she said. This was definitely a delusion, a sign her mind was beginning to snap. The Queen's tentacles were only a few centimeters away from Hanabi.

Something flew out of the sky, landing between them. It was made of something black and gleaming, a powerful, durable, hardened material designed to absorb magic. It was the same Ultra Magic Hardened Blade widely used in Sixth Generation Division

Maneuvers. Every living creature on the battlefield looked up. By the time they had, the Cavalleria was already yanking the Blade back out of the ground, having slipped right through their fields of view. The only one who saw him clearly was Hanabi.

Activate Armament:

The little Cavalleria raised his Blade toward the sky. This was an art he shouldn't have been able to use. He didn't have enough magic to do so, and the magic you were born with could never change. Hanabi knew this, but she also knew of a means to break through the limits of talent. She heard him whisper the words:

Nine-Count Strike.

The backpack on Soukyu (Pleiades) opened. Nine arms extended in a fan-shaped pattern, gleaming like a sun behind it. Those arms were a unique weapon inherited from Kuon's master, a precious treasure customized for him alone. In the corner of Hanabi's vision, a magic gauge with Kuon's name on it began rising like a mad thing. By the time the Jave's attention was on him, it had stopped at 999,999. Hanabi knew the weapon could turn him into a Division 5 for nine seconds, but she had no idea combining it with the Shichisei Kenbu methods to enhance one's magic in a DM could achieve a number like that.

Kishin.

The sun on the DM's back grew bright, as if igniting. The heat from the magic exhaust alone vaporized the tentacles and minor Jave around Hanabi. Kuon's bubble protected the three Fuji Squad members, who remained frozen to the spot, staring at the little Cavalleria.

"Ryuenbu!"

A wind blew, as strong as a storm—*no, a tornado,* Hanabi amended herself.

Kuon was at the center of the tornado that covered the entire battlefield. A terrifying ring of violent winds began blowing everything away. Disk-shaped guillotines, each the size of a Jave, spun like mad within the winds. Kuon had used Tensetsu to pinpoint the locations of friend and foe alike before unleashing an attack which never harmed a hair on the squad's heads, while exterminating the monsters. The tornado sliced and diced, mowing down everything in its path. A merciless trail of body parts was left in its wake, but to Hanabi it seemed like the sweetest wind that had ever blown.

It was just like that day. The same wind that had blown back then...

It was over in a moment. All that remained of the monsters around them was a red mist and a deathly silence. The distinctive scent left by powerful magic beams filled Hanabi's nostrils. The blue bubble protecting them was gone, having shielded them from that terrifying wind attack.

She looked at Kuon, dazed. The nine arms deployed at his back retracted, but Hanabi was unaware this meant the special weapon had stopped functioning.

Hanabi just thought, *But he's dead.* Yet the Hero who had died thirteen years ago was right there in front of her.

Without turning to face her, he spoke to Hanabi in that exact same tone: "I'm glad you survived." It was like he'd been waiting thirteen years to say that to her. "I'm glad you lived to grow up. That was my last wish."

The Hero turned around. By then, his features had become something much more familiar. Maybe it had just been a dream, perhaps an illusion, but the idea was real.

My little Hero is right here...

"Sorry I kept you waiting, Hanabi-senpai."

It was Okegawa Kuon.

He'd come. She had no words.

The fight was over. Hanabi was crying like a child. All the air in her lungs rushed out in a giant sob as she inhaled great gasps of spent magic and dark red mist to replace it.

In the center of the scorched earth battlefield, Kuon reduced his DM to minimal deployment and put his arms around Hanabi. He stroked her head as she clung to him with all her might. "Sorry I took so long, senpai. I made it in time though. Thank goodness."

Hanabi took a long whiff of his scent and shook her head. Her answer didn't make it into words, but Kuon understood what she was trying to say: *I thought you weren't coming. How dare you take so long? But I believed in you. I was so scared. So very scared. But you came. I'm so happy. Thank you. I'm so glad to see you. But what took so long, you idiot? You're an idiot. I love you.*

So Kuon just said, "Yes, yes, sorry," and Hanabi was glad for that. She rubbed her face on his scrawny chest, still sobbing.

"Senpai, I brought some spare capsules for everyone." Kuon took a small plastic box out of his pocket and showed it to Hanabi.

She accepted it, and the moment she released him he went over to Fuji and Rin, giving them capsules as well. "Let's use these to get out of here. There are ships out to—"

Kuon's words died in his mouth. The blood drained from his face.

"Kuon-sama!" En shrieked.

"I know!" he yelled, turning around. His senpai looked confused, but Kuon and his Guide were focused on one thing: the hole hanging above them at the Gate.

"Senpai! Run—"

The hole expanded.

Everything around them turned pitch black in every direction. They found themselves floating in space with only the tiny lights of the stars in the distance.

"Senpai?!"

Tentacles wrapped around her, and... "Kuon-kun! No! Kuon-kun!!"

"Senpai!" Kuon reached out his hand, but there was a jerk, and Hanabi and the tentacles sank into the void.

"Hanabi!"

"Suzuka-kun!"

Deploying their DMs, all three looked around, searching for Hanabi. But there was no sign of her. They couldn't see her anywhere.

It was very quiet, almost like they were floating in the depths of the sea again.

"En! Find her, please! And hurry!"

"I am!"

If he were to blindly trust his radar, speedometer, altimeter, and magic meter, right now, they were inside a bubble of magic with a value of 7,777,777 while traveling at three times the speed of light at an altitude of -5000 meters. In Kuon's previous life, En hadn't been with him, but now she confirmed those readings to be somehow correct.

Damn it! I was right there with her!

Kuon gritted his teeth, swearing. Hanabi had to be there somewhere. When he'd seen his squadmates surrounded by Jave and the Queen in the sky, Kuon had resolved to finish them all off in a single attack. He may not have learned the ultimate art, but his magic expenditure had already sunk to 1/100,000,000. He figured if he used Nine-Count Strike, he could pull off the strongest art he'd used in his previous life, so long as it was within that nine-second window.

His attempt had failed.

I never thought the Queen would return so soon!

He'd blown away all the ordinary Jave, just like last time, but it had never occurred to him it would cause the Gate to go haywire and swallow them up.

Kuon realized the four flesh pillars weren't Gate control devices. At the bitter end of his past life, the Queen had tried to eat him without killing him first. Since the Queen had been badly injured, the Gate went ten years without opening. The field inside the Gate had a magic value of 7,777,777, which could be classified as Division 7, and he guessed this was itself

magically activated...just like Division Maneuvers. And Division
Maneuvers were weapons you wore with magic—in a sense, putting one on was like casting a spell.

In which case, that meant the Gate was essentially a DM the
Jave used. Like the invisible bullets they utilized, it was a magic spell.

The high-end AI Device, En, agreed with this assessment. So
what was it that activated the Gate? Not those four flesh pillars.
What kind of creature could put out a number as ridiculous as
7,777,777? Kuon could only think of one.

"Kuon-sama! There!" En pointed.

"What? Below us?!"

All three piloted their frames in the direction En indicated.
The monster they found there had soaked the blow from Kishin
Ryuenbu, oozing thick, black blood, but stubbornly clinging to
life. It was the big boss of all the monsters.

The Jave Queen.

When she saw Kuon coming, she spread her tentacles like a
wild animal trying to make itself look bigger.

"Hanabi-sama's signal is inside that Core!" En shouted.

He'd seen that Core during the fight in his past life, after it
had failed to swallow him and fled to the other world. That glowing purple eye... This time, it had obtained the ultimate meal, and
taken it inside itself.

He checked again at maximum magnification. Inside that
purple orb, he saw Hanabi bound by countless tentacles. Her eyes
opened.

"Senpai!"

"Kuon-kun...?"

Their comms still worked; Hanabi was still alive. "Just you wait! I'm coming to save you!" Kuon drew his Blade and charged. Rin and Fuji expanded their DMs, giving chase.

Skreeeaaaaaaaaa!

The Queen put up a final resistance. An incredible number of tentacles thrashed. Kuon could swing his Blade, but couldn't cut through them all. The ones suddenly appearing from empty space were particularly obnoxious. His radar was just barely picking them up in time, but he still couldn't force his way any closer to the Queen.

Fuji and Rin weren't faring any better. The capsules had recovered their magic a little, but not nearly enough for them to fight properly. "Damn it!" "Hanabi!" they swore over the comms.

Kuon was in much worse condition. He'd already lost his extra boosters, and his magic was almost entirely tapped out.

But if I have three more seconds...

He had only used Nine-Count Strike for six; he still had three seconds left.

Unless he got closer, he couldn't use any short-ranged attacks. An area attack like Ryuenbu wouldn't get him anywhere either. To beat the Queen, he needed an art that would focus all his output on a single point—his strongest art.

Shijin Reppakuzan... But...but that...

Reppakuzan could kill this thing. In his previous life, it had left the Queen on the brink of death. In her current condition, that art would finish her.

But if he used that, it would take Hanabi out with it. That wasn't an option.

Kuon's hesitation made his movements falter. The Queen's hundreds of mouths blinked, firing an untold number of bullets.

"Tch!" Faced with a barrage even Tensetsu couldn't get him through, Kuon forced his mind to think.

Think! There must be a way!

But the Queen's injuries were visibly healing. She was draining Hanabi's magic.

Then En screamed, "This... That movement... It can't be!"

The space behind the Queen warped. All the numbers En had been monitoring rapidly began shifting. This closely resembled the readings just before the Gate opened in their world. En knew what that meant.

"Kuon-sama! The enemy's getting ready to run!"

"Ah!"

"If you don't stop it, it... It'll take Hanabi-sama with it!"

"I won't let that happen!" Dodging the bullets, Kuon desperately tried closing the distance. But his body felt sluggish, his frame heavy. His magic, his speed, his specs, this Division 1 frame—none of it was good enough. Without his talent, he couldn't save Hanabi.

Tentacles popped out of empty space. He was unable to dodge in time and they sliced his side, drawing blood. He screamed. "Hanabi-senpai!"

Trapped inside that orb, Hanabi's lips parted, her words faltering. "What...are you waiting for?" she asked, like she was accusing him of something. Her face was pallid. "Hurry up and fire."

Those words told Kuon everything. Hanabi was already certain she was dying. As a soldier, as a Cavalleria, she had chosen the Jave Queen's defeat over her own life.

"Senpai!"

If the Queen fled here, the Gate would be sealed, but only temporarily. The same thing would happen in another ten years. No, these monsters were clever. If the Queen absorbed Hanabi, she would obtain not only Hanabi's powerful magic, but Hanabi's memories of DM research. This time, she would conquer mankind for good, obtaining lasting control.

He had to kill the Queen here, even at the cost of a Maneuver Cavalleria's life.

Hanabi's life for the future of humanity. Hanabi herself had already accepted that. She accepted it the night before she was deployed, the night she had spent with Kuon.

There was no need to hesitate. But...

"Sorry..." Hanabi said. "Goodbye, Kuon-kun. If... If I'm reborn..."

She smiled.

"I hope I see you again..."

That was her goodbye. Hanabi would be like the Hero she admired, giving her life to save mankind. She was ready for it. She thought it was the right thing to do.

She was the only one who did.

Kuon stopped time for a second. In that soundless, negative world, she saw him staring directly at her. His eyes said everything. There was a rage in them that scared her.

To hell with that, they said. *I'm not gonna let that happen!*

The man who'd been the Hero, who threw his own life away just like Hanabi was about to, was astonished by the strength of his reaction.

"Rraggghhhhhhhhhhhhhhhhhhhhhhhhhh!" Kuon roared. Behind him, Rin and Fuji watched helplessly.

"Okegawa-kun?!"

"Kyuu-kun!"

Kuon charged forward. If he couldn't use Ryuenbu, then he would just have to slice open that Core and pull Hanabi out himself. Who cared if he didn't have the magic or talent? He wasn't about to let a reason like that, the unfair facts of his birth, be an excuse to let her make herself a lone hero.

Not over Jogen or the capital or in the deep sea, but here, in the Gate, covered in wounds, Kuon blocked the tentacle attacks. He flew toward Hanabi, refusing to give up. Bullets and tentacles he couldn't quite dodge tore at his frame and flesh. Still, he pressed on. Okegawa Kuon would never turn back from saving Suzuka Hanabi.

"You don't get to make that choice for us!" he shouted. Tears streamed down his face as he charged in. Kuon couldn't shoot Hanabi. He wouldn't, couldn't ever do it. He could throw away his own life in a heartbeat because that was how he'd always lived, and how he'd died once already. But that only applied to him.

"Hanabi-senpai! I...!"

The girl he'd saved at the end of his previous life, whom he'd looked up to, respected, and fallen in love with? He couldn't let her make that sacrifice. Not ever. The rage he felt at the very idea shocked him. It had taken control. He realized for the first time this was how his master had felt.

"I won't let you do that!"

Kuon's mind, body, and magic all completely rejected the notion. To save Hanabi here was tantamount to destroying the world. He knew that. He understood it.

But he couldn't leave her. He didn't want to. He wouldn't let himself.

The armor on his left shoulder was torn off. He had almost no feeling left in his right leg, but he didn't let that stop him. "Saving the world at the cost of a life?" he yelled at Hanabi. Then he said the same words his master had used: *"We don't need a Hero like that!"*

That was the answer.

In that moment, he thought he saw something. At the center of the magic around him, deep within his DM's Core, he saw a flash of light.

Ah!

It wasn't clear what exactly allowed Kuon to understand what that light was. It wasn't his mind, his body, or his magic that did it. Perhaps it was the accumulated wisdom of his arts, of his sword, that allowed him to understand that this, this right here, was something you could only see once you'd answered Shichisei Kenbu's final question.

This was what his master called the "light of life."

A ray of light rose up in the back of Kuon's mind as he let his anger carry him blindly forward. This was a clear and present path to saving Hanabi—a path trod not by a Hero, but by a boy with almost no magic.

"Squad Leader, Control!"

On standby behind him, the Cavalleria who led the school's best squad got it right away. "Huh?! Roger that! Motegi-kun, support him!" Fuji responded.

"I don't get it, but okay!"

Hearing his senpai's voices behind him, Kuon upped his speed. He didn't have enough magic left to use Tensetsu to see the future. Using the enemy position data Fuji had calculated and the approach routes En was crunching together, he pressed on through the mass of tentacles and the hail of invisible bullets. The sparks flashing before his strained eyes showed Rin was shooting down any attacks he couldn't dodge. With the help of the companions he'd lacked in his former life, for the sake of the one he loved in this one, the Division 1 Cavalleria charged at the monster boss.

The Queen loomed large. He could clearly see Hanabi in her cell. "Senpai!" he called.

Kuon didn't care if he died. This wasn't suicide or heroism. Sixty percent of his frame's functions had ceased and the only limb he could properly move was his left arm. The bullets that had penetrated the barrier weren't fatal, but they'd left him covered in wounds, and his body was burning up. Even though he was covered in blood and cuts, with no magic left, if he could save the person he loved, then Kuon didn't care if he died doing it.

Hanabi stared back at him, sobbing. "Kuon-kun! Kuon-kun! Why? Why?!" Even as her expression scolded him for not shooting her, for placing her life on the scale opposite all mankind and making such a stupid choice…

"Why do you always come?!"

Kuon heard a glimmer of hope and joy behind her question. "I won't ever let you be alone again!"

His radar was still active, displaying enemy coordinates with precision. The alarms sounded. A moment later, countless spear-like tentacles shot out of empty space.

"Nine-Count Strike!"

With only three seconds left, Kuon deployed his special weapon, raising his magic to Division 5. He activated Tensetsu as he did, slowing his sense of time and searching for evasion routes. There were none; of course not. He had no use for evasion routes now. If it meant saving Suzuka Hanabi, Okegawa Kuon would never turn back.

He could only go forward.

Kuon reached the Queen, leaving all the enemy attacks behind in his wake. His body instinctively shifted into the Shimetsu form, the same form he'd used as the final art when he first met Hanabi, and Hanabi's and his hearts connected in combat.

"Now, Kuon-sama!" En yelled. En was a high-spec AI Device powered by his master's magic, a reflection of her will that was here to monitor him. She chose this moment to tell Kuon what he needed to know. "The ultimate art of Shichisei Kenbu is called…"

Kuon focused on the Queen's Core, exposed when she had failed to swallow him in his previous life and fled into this dimension. That Core had captured Hanabi and was draining her magic. There was something else behind it—a Nova Kuon hadn't previously perceived.

Shichisei Kenbu Ultimate Art: Mumyo Tosen.

His sword flashed.

The Blade Kuon thrust forward struck what appeared to be an ordinary wall of flesh, an arbitrary part of the Jave Queen. But with Kuon's magic raised to Division 5 and the full force of that magic charging his Ultra Magic Hardened Blade, the blow triggered a baffling reaction in the fleshy monster.

Magic power flooded every part of the Queen's and Kuon's bodies. The magic pooled on the Queen's skin sent ripples running through the rest of her body, and Kuon's Mumyo Tosen focused all his magic into the pure light of life.

Kuon's body knew all too well what concentrated magic would do. Usually, magic brought to the critical compression threshold would try expanding, directing its force outward. However, the magic focused by Mumyo Tosen reflected against itself, unable to go anywhere, and the breath of death known as Magic Dispersal began blowing within the Jave Queen.

This was the same Magic Dispersal he'd used to blow himself up in his past life, but it now tore his enemy's body to pieces. Mumyo Tosen was unstoppable, a fatal blow that forced his enemy's magic to self-destruct.

Skreeeeeeeeeeeeeeeeeeeeeeeeeee!

The Queen's tentacles whipped around, convulsing. A moment later, the Core cracked open. Kuon grabbed Hanabi and retreated with her in his arms, the Queen's scream echoing in his ears. That final scream shook the entire space inside the Gate, a cry of rage and loathing and sadness. Even Kuon, who'd once connected with the Queen's magic, didn't know what that scream really meant.

"I didn't think I'd hear a voice like that from you," he said as he watched the Queen disintegrate. "But sorry. I—*we* still want to live."

The Queen dissolved before his eyes as the Gate which allowed her to cross to the other side opened. With no magic left, Kuon and Hanabi were pulled into it, along with chunks of the Queen's flesh.

It was a quiet place, like the depths of the sea. Two Division Maneuvers floated through it. In Kuon's arms, Hanabi groaned. Her eyes opened. "Kuon...kun...?"

"How are you feeling, Hanabi-senpai?" Kuon said, smiling at her.

"Ah!"

She just threw her arms around him wordlessly, crying.

"I'm really glad you're safe," he said, stroking her head. He was genuinely relieved. En had already examined her condition: She was almost out of magic, but otherwise unharmed.

Hanabi cried for a while, but then she frowned and pinched Kuon's cheeks hard.

"Mmphhhhhh?!"

"That's for not shooting when I told you to shoot!"

"Mmmph mmmphhhmphhh."

"I know. That's why..." She stopped yanking his cheeks and threw her arms around him. Then she leaned in for a kiss.

"Um...er...is this...?" He felt himself blushing.

Hanabi smiled. "That's for choosing me."

"You're welcome..."

"I love you, my Hero." She smiled and put her lips on his again.

"Erm. Ahem! Ahem!" En appeared next to them, making a great show of clearing her throat.

"Eeep! Since when were you here, En-kun?"

"Since always? The whole time?"

"You're bad for the heart, seriously."

"Much as I would love to trade barbs with you all day, do you realize where we are?"

Hanabi looked around. "Uh...good question."

"We're still inside the Gate," Kuon said. "En, do you know what's going on? Are we being sucked into the Jave world?"

"No," his Guide said, shaking her head. "The Queen was maintaining the Gate, and with her destruction, there wasn't enough magic left to transport us. This is merely conjecture, but I imagine we will be returned to our own world safely. However..."

"What?"

"There is no guarantee we'll be returned at the same time, and there is a possibility you'll be forced to abandon your bodies and send your souls back alone."

"I wouldn't qualify that as returning safely..."

"Our souls?" Hanabi asked. "What does that mean?"

"Your memories will be transplanted into a baby somewhere. Essentially, you'll be reincarnated."

"Reincarnated...?"

"God only knows where. It'll all sort itself out, I'm sure. You'll just have to pray your bodies go back with you I suppose."

Kuon sighed. His hands tightened around Hanabi.

"It'll be okay, Kuon-kun," she said.

"I hope so."

"I'm sure of it. Even if we are reincarnated..." Hanabi gave him another kiss and smiled. "I'm sure we'll find each other again."

Her smile nearly blinded Kuon. The girl he'd met at the end of his last life had grown up to be so beautiful. She'd saved him as well, and they'd fallen in love.

"You won't ever leave me alone, will you?" she asked.

Kuon smiled back. "Not ever."

Maybe he was about to start a third life. That itself wasn't frightening. He knew they'd meet again.

The Gate began crumbling, light enveloping them in the place they lost consciousness.

BACK ON EARTH, medals were given to a Cavalleria squad.

Student Echelon Supporting Retreat Destroys Gate, screamed the newspapers. The accompanying photo showed a serious, handsome boy, and a warm-hearted girl with glasses.

Just those two.

The Gate over the capital had vanished. There were still several Gates scattered around the Empire, but recovering the capital, the heart of the Empire, was huge—even if the furious battle had turned it into scorched earth. Not only the Empire, but every world government was working together, trying to close all Gates on Earth.

The second semester had begun at Jogen Maneuver Academy. The freshly decorated Lunatic Order received even more attention than before, becoming a model for the entire student body. The always serious squad leader merely said, "We'll have to work even harder than before."

The quirky subleader refused to say anything but, "What a pain, what a pain, what a pain." The squad leader and his fiancée were doing very well, and the subleader had gotten a haircut and new glasses. The squad leader asked (unnecessarily) why she didn't try wearing contacts. She gave an exasperated sigh and said it would lose her the few fans she had.

It was just the two of them. With her new haircut fluttering in the breeze, the subleader looked up at the skies over Jogen. "We can't even do a mock battle, Hanabi."

The Maneuver Cavalleria were out hunting Jave again. The school hadn't lost a single student since the previous operation ended. Mankind had entered a time of comparative peace.

There was no longer just one lone Hero.

_//////////⌐

Watching the news, a certain high-end AI Device Guide reported to her new master. "Hey! This one, too! They aren't showing our two Heroes!"

"No, that's good. I mean, senpai and I were both so out of magic we've been stuck in bed until just recently."

"And just whose bed were you in?" En asked.

"What are you implying?! Hospital beds! Separate ones!"

"Oh? You think I don't know about all your nightly trysts?"

"We didn't have any! Look, you're tied to my magic now, so I *will* put you in Sleep Mode."

"Ohhh, sowwwy, Masterrr." The fairy Guide rubbed up against her master. She wore a uniform that looked like a modified silk kimono. It sort of reminded him of the female conductors on local train lines.

The one she called "Master" was enjoying his first walk to school in several days. He was deliberately very early, both to avoid the extra attention the medals had brought them, and also so he could meet his girlfriend.

Jogen Academy had a large dorm. A beautiful girl with a long black ponytail and a far curvier figure than most schoolgirls commanded was waiting at the entrance, radiating nobility. *The Warrior Princess,* he thought, smiling. He called out to her. She smiled back happily, and he'd never seen anything lovelier. "Good morning, Hanabi-senpai," he greeted her.

"Mm, morning, Kuon-kun."

Okegawa Kuon and Suzuka Hanabi, the two Heroes who'd destroyed the Gate, were about to begin their first day back at school.

Watching them chatting happily as they walked, En said, "By the way, Master, Hanabi-sama."

"What?"

"Yes?"

"When's the wedding?"

Both hung their heads. *They have a long road ahead of them,* En thought. She sighed, staring up at the sky.

It was as blue as her master's frame.

DIVISIONMANEUVER

NICE TO MEET YOU ALL. I'm Shippo Senoo. This is my first book, and my first afterword.

First, some thanks.

To my editor, Kurita-san, thank you for all your help getting this book published.

The illustrations were done by Nidy-2D-san, whom I'd wanted to have do the illustrations even before I won this prize. My dream was granted. Kuon, Hanabi, the Master, and En all turned out so adorable and cool. I am incredibly grateful Nidy-2D-san took the job despite being so busy. Thank you so much.

To my Twitter friends, Senya-san, Kirin-san, Gunsou, Konodera-san, Manabu-san, and all my wannabe friends, thank you for reading things before submission. Thanks for believing I'd win more than I ever did. If Nagashima-sensei reads this, please treat yourself to some great German food.

Thank you to everyone involved with the publication, and most of all, to anyone who picked up this book.

I am so thankful I could easily fill this entire afterword with gratitude.

What did you think of *Division Maneuver: Vol. 1*?

This went through several revisions between winning the 6th Kodansha Lanove Bunko New Writer Prize. This is my first work as a writer.

The earlier version of this story was set in space, on one of nine lunar colonies in orbit around the Earth, but, after revising it, the setting changed to Earth itself.

As a result, you get to see Hanabi-senpai end up wearing a string bikini on a south seas island beach, so I think this was the right choice.

Those of you who are motorcycle fans may notice the character names are all taken from circuits in Japan.

Suzuka, Motegi, Fuji, Tsukuba, Okegawa... There are so many of them, but as a Honda guy, my favorite is the Suzuka Circuit.

The fireworks at the end of the Suzuka 8 Hours are fantastic. The NSR is the greatest machine of my biking life. The En Nidy-2D- drew is far too cute.

So, in other good news, I also won a prize from Shueisha-san. There's no release date over there yet, but there are some connections between that story and *Division Maneuver,* so I hope you'll look forward to it.

I hope we can meet again in the near future.

Thank you for reading all this way.

—Shippo Senoo

SHIPPO SENOO

A Libra, born in 1982. Began writing novels at the age of ten, jumped ship to screenplays, won an anime screenwriting contest and got a job at a game company, but still loved novels so went back to light novels like a total flirt. After four years of writing, he finally won and did so at both Kodansha-san and Shueisha-san's contests at once—a double prize! Pretty sure he's used up his entire life's worth of luck. He'll try to live strong.

NIDY-2D-

Illustrator. Primarily for games like *Phantasy Star Online 2es* and *Gunslinger Stratos,* but also TCG and light novel illustrations and designs. Particularly good at mechagirls—drawings of girls fused with machines.

DIVISIONMANEUVER